KU-677-401

USBORNE

The Last Circus Tiger

By Claire Barker   Illustrated by Ross Collins

Contents

Chapter 1

PLAYING DEAD

Starcross Hall was Knitbone Pepper's idea of Heaven. Hiding down a grassy lane in Bartonshire, England, it had spelled H-O-M-E for generations of the Pepper family – both people and pets – for the last 904 years.

The tumbledown house had snoozed away the centuries, hugged by ivy and soothed by birdsong. Within its crumbling walls and rickety towers, there were interesting secrets; secrets that scampered round corners, waddled down its echoing corridors and pattered through the half-abandoned rooms.

Normal house rules did not apply at Starcross Hall. Nobody ever said "Tidy up" or "Where are you going with that catapult?" No game was ever too noisy, too mad or too messy. It was never too late, or too early or too *anything* to play. It was the best adventure playground in the world and dogs were definitely allowed in. *Especially* ghost dogs.

Knitbone Pepper lay in the darkness of Winnie's bedroom, waiting inside the wardrobe with his paws over his eyes, counting to himself as patiently as he could. Hide-and-seek was his favourite game because it involved all the things that dogs liked doing best, i.e. sniffing, finding, chasing and fetching. He wiggled his eyebrows and gave his nose a thoughtful lick.

To pass the time, Knitbone worked on his strategy which, as he knew the other ghosts' favourite hiding places like the back of his paw, didn't take very long.

Martin was bound to be in the biscuit tin, giving himself away with hamstery crunching and munching noises. Gabriel the goose would be perched on the top shelf in the library, squeezed next to the encyclopaedias. What about Valentine? A hare, he'd be lying low in the shady space under the big hedge in the courtyard. Orlando would be monkeying around in the kitchen cutlery drawer, clattering about amongst the spoons.

That just left wonderful Winnie Pepper. Knitbone was certain that she was the best and cleverest human person in the whole world, but even *she* couldn't hide from her beloved ghost dog.

This was for three reasons:

1. They'd been playing hide-and-seek all Winnie's life (and some of Knitbone's death) and he never lost.

2. She smelled nicer than anything else in Heaven and earth so was easy to track down because her scent bowled down the corridors like clouds.

3. She was the only one in the group of friends who was a) human and b) still alive. Both of these things meant that she was very solid and was easier to spot than a frozen pea in an ice cube.

"Sixteen…seventeen…eighteennineteen TWENTY!" Knitbone shot out of the wardrobe, across Winnie's bedroom and raced down the dusty corridor howling, "COMING! READY OR NOT!"

Galloping down the sweeping Starcross staircase, Knitbone momentarily remembered that, once upon a time, he had been very sad. But now Winnie could see him again, his days whizzed by in a blur of doggy joy. Knitbone was Winnie's "Beloved": an extra-special ghost pet and her best friend for ever. His afterlife was dead good and he never, ever wanted things to change.

Chapter 2

THE POWER
OF A
POSiTiVE
HATTiTUDE

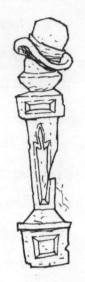

"EVERYTHING IS GOING TO CHANGE!"
The very next morning, Winnie's
dad, the 18th Lord of Starcross, burst through
the kitchen door, his eyes wide and his hair
standing on end. He thrust his arms in the
air, knocking down a copper pan with a loud
clatter.

Astonished, Lady Pepper put her honey
crumpet down. Winnie stopped eating her
cereal, spoon halfway to her mouth. Knitbone,

sitting next to Winnie and invisible to the grown-ups, looked horrified.

"Last night I had a dream," Lord Pepper continued, his cheeks pink and eyebrows waggling wildly, "that Starcross Hall was home to the largest hat collection *IN THE WORLD!*" He looked at his wife. "Oh, Isadora, it was so beautiful…you would have loved it. Shiny crowns, glossy bearskins, nightcaps with fluffy pompoms…" He sighed wistfully. "Then I woke up."

"Our private collection is splendid, of course," he said, gesturing at the towering piles of hats that lay around the kitchen, "but the undeniable fact is *this*: you simply can't have too many hats."

Lord Pepper began to pace around the kitchen, tapping his forehead. "*Then* I thought to myself, *Hang on a minute, Hector Augustus Merriweather Pepper, what better way to spend money than by buying even more hats?* Ha! It's so obvious! Hats are where it's at. Everybody's 'hat' it! Look!"

He held up the latest copy of *Mad Hatter Monthly*, his favourite magazine. On its cover was a glossy photograph of a yellow turban adorned with a glittering red ruby brooch the size of a potato. The headline read:

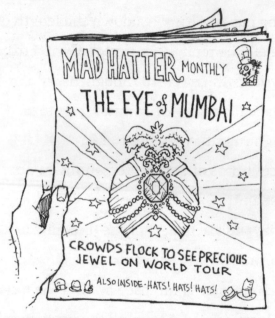

Lord Pepper continued pacing. "I've got big, big plans. It's time to get in on the act – we must expand our collection and open to the public!" He reached into his dressing-gown pocket and pulled out a jester's hat, planting it firmly on his head. "It's our destiny! The dream was a SIGN!"

He sat down on a kitchen chair with a plonk. Having never expressed this much ambition in his whole life, he was now worn out. Lady P slid a soothing cup of turnip tea down the length of the table and he took a long restorative slurp.

Everyone was quiet and thought about Lord Pepper's idea for a moment. Even the other Beloved ghosts sitting under the kitchen table, used to centuries of Pepper peculiarities, stopped playing snap.

Winnie was the first to break the silence. "Dad, are you saying that you want visitors to come to Starcross?" She cast a doubtful eye at the cobwebs in the corners and the dusty hats on the floor. "Actual tourists? To come here?"

Her father nodded, restored by the miracle of turnip tea. "It's time for a new start, Winnie. All that dreadful auction business – nearly losing the dear old place – has made me realize that Starcross has been sleeping for far too long. It *is* the twenty-first century, you know! Lots and lots of visitors coming to see lots and lots of HATS – that's what we need! People; smiling, jolly, happy people! Putting Starcross Hall on the map once more – it'll be a smashing day out for all ages!" His words came tumbling like bonbons from a jar, "My head feels like it's exploding with ideas for the first time in years." He sprang back up onto his feet and did a little pirouette.

"It'll be more fun than a pocketful of frogs. Isadora, what do you say, old girl?"

Lady P stood to attention, her thoughts clicking into place. "But, Hector, that would mean… *we would have jobs!*" Her mouth fell open. "Actual JOBS! What a brilliant idea! I've always wanted a *job*." She pondered for a moment and then gasped, clutching at her feather boa. "Of course – my new oven! All those visitors will be hungry after looking at all the marvellous hats. I have always dreamed of opening my own cafe!" She began to pace around the kitchen, her eyebrows knitted together. "Somewhere that I could show off my boldest, most adventurous recipes. I could call it… *The Burpy Buffet.* Hang on… *The Belly Deli…* No… *Pantry Pirates* – that's it!"

Lord and Lady Pepper climbed onto the table and danced a wild polka, swinging from the stag-antler chandelier, cheering and whooping with joy.

They were having such a great time they didn't

notice that Winnie had trailed out of the kitchen, opened the front door and left for school, a ghostly ribbon of invisible animals in tow.

"Well," huffed Knitbone as he and the other Spirits of Starcross followed Winnie up the lane to the bus stop. "I'm not sure about this at all, no I'm not. It all sounds very risky." He launched into a full-blown rant. "I don't like the idea of lots of people coming and going. What if they get in the way of our games, or…or stop our Keep Fit sessions? I don't want to go back to being a weak and flabby phantom. I like things exactly as they are. No, it's definitely a Bad Idea. In fact, it's a Terrible Idea, and that's the end of the matter." He growled to underline his point.

Winnie patted him on the head. "Don't worry, Knitbone, it might be a good thing. It's tradition, anyway. Starcross always used to have lots of visitors, didn't it, Gabriel?"

Gabriel the goose honked in agreement as he waddled along, kicking the weeds growing in the middle of the road. "Oh-yes-oh-yes-oh-yes, it certainly-certainly did."

Valentine the hare hopped along next to Winnie. "Hundreds of years ago parties and feasts used to happen here all the time."

Excited, Orlando the Elizabethan monkey jumped up onto her shoulder. "Oh! Oh! Once we had a beeg, beeg celebration with lions and tigers and snugglers…"

Winnie giggled as she walked. "Snugglers?"

Valentine rolled his eyes. "He means jugglers."

Martin the hamster was panting heavily as he ran alongside, trying to keep up with everyone else. "At the end of the Second World War," he gasped, "we had a party. Everybody in Bartonshire came. I ate a dodgy Scotch egg. Then I died."

"You see?" whined Knitbone, scampering

backwards in front of Winnie, his eyes like saucers. "Did you hear that? Martin actually *died*. It's not safe. Why can't it just be us? We're happy as we are, aren't we? It's nearly the summer holidays and I've been looking forward to them for ages! Why can't everything *just stay the same*?"

They reached the top of the lane just as the school bus drew up. Winnie kneeled down and stroked Knitbone's ears, trying to soothe his anxiousness. "*Because*, Knitbone Pepper, dear old Beloved, change is sometimes a good thing. And you never know, it might actually be fun!"

Winnie clambered up onto the bus, took her seat and huffed hot breath onto the cool window. She drew a heart in the disappearing mist with her finger and blew Knitbone a kiss, unaware of the driver watching her in his rear-view mirror. *That Winnie Pepper certainly is an odd one,* he thought to himself, pulling away from the bus stop.

Chapter 3

HAT HAVOC

Back at Starcross, Lord Pepper wasted no time in making his dream come true. It was as if all of the years he had spent pootling about had been in preparation for this mission. He spent every waking moment poring over the well-thumbed pages of *Mad Hatter Monthly*, circling all the hats he wanted to buy in red pen. He sat for hours in the library, going through reference books, four pairs of forgotten reading glasses balanced on top of his head, writing a

very, *very* long shopping list of wild headgear
to add to their already overflowing collection.

Consequently, it wasn't long before hats began
to arrive. Lorry after lorry, van after van, rumbled
into the Starcross courtyard. Big boxes, small
boxes, tall boxes and squat boxes, thin boxes, fat
boxes and very, very square boxes. Some came in
candy-coloured stripy cartons and others came
in black lacquered chests. They came in sacks,
they came in crates, they came in trunks. Some
were tied with shiny silk ribbons, some were
buckled firmly with thick brown leather straps.
By the first Thursday of the school summer
holidays, the Peppers were knee-deep in
headgear – bonnets, cowboy hats,
pointy princess things with long
flowing veils, Roman helmets
and cavalier hats with ostrich
feather plumes. It was like a hat
avalanche had landed on Starcross.

Privately,
Winnie had expected
her parents' project
to be nothing more than
another of their short-lived
madcap ideas, like the time badgers
were allowed to live in the ballroom,
or when they tried to genetically
engineer a butterbee. But this was
looking like something altogether more
serious.

"Dad, where will we put them all?"
worried Winnie, as she accidentally stepped
on a tiara. "We are drowning in hats!"

"And a jolly good job too, I'd say." Lord P waved in the direction of the calendar on the wall. To her horror Winnie noticed that there was a big red circle drawn around the following Monday. "Did I mention that we are opening to the public in four days?"

Winnie was speechless. Catching sight of her expression, Lord Pepper patted her happily on the head. "Don't worry, darling. It's all going to be *absolutely smashing*. Could you mention the good news to your mother?"

Lady Pepper was busy in the garden, snipping leaves off this and that, tasting them and spitting bits out again. She had been spending hours at the kitchen table devising increasingly bizarre recipes for the cafe menu.

Winnie burst through the kitchen doors and into the garden, trying to remain calm. "Dad says we are opening on Monday! That's in four days' time! FOUR DAYS! Isn't that a bit soon?" Winnie cast an anxious eye around. In the corner was a rusty Victorian bath, overflowing with weeds, snails meandering down the sides. The centrepiece of the garden was an ancient marble statue; a family of blackbirds nesting where its head should have been. "Do you think Starcross could do with a bit of tidying first?"

"What? Hmm? Monday?" Lady P asked absent-mindedly, putting down her shears and wandering back into the kitchen. "Yes, dear, if you want, Monday sounds perfect. My cafe is ready to swing into action. The freezer is already packed with delicious and challenging delights. Now, taste this!" Winnie's mother had seized a wooden spoon from a bubbling pot and was waving it in her direction. A greyish sauce glooped off the end and Winnie reluctantly touched it with the tip of her tongue. To her surprise it wasn't too bad.

"Can you taste a hint of mint?" Lady P asked.

"Can you taste a sparkle of lemon?" Winnie nodded. Her mother scribbled it down in her recipe book. Then she pushed her glasses up her nose, "What about the smidgeon of pigeon?"

Winnie spluttered into the sink.

"Alas, pigeon fails again." Lady P recorded this in her journal, before turning back to the stove. "Winnie, what about this one?"

But Winnie was already gone, sprinting up the stairs.

"Winnie!" As she pushed open the attic door, Knitbone bounded over to her, licking her face. "Are you here to see us do our workout? Got to keep fighting fit! Do you want to do some dancing?" He wrinkled his nose. "Why do you taste of pigeon?"

Gabriel was standing on one leg wearing a T-shirt that said "Fabulous Phantom" and munching a beakful of ginger biscuits.

"Snack, Winnie?"
he honked, spraying
crumbs over his
yoga mat.

"Thank you,"
sighed Winnie,
sitting down on the rug
and taking a biscuit
from the half-empty
packet.

"Erm...to be absolutely
correct, Winnie," Martin piped up, "whilst you
are an honorary member of Spirits Of Starcross,
you're not *actually* a ghost, are you? So, as an
actual ghost, I can look after that biscuit for you,
if you want..."

Winnie smiled and handed her ginger biscuit
to the hopeful hamster.

"I'll just put it over here for safekeeping..."
Martin disappeared with it behind a cupboard.

There was a muffled crunching sound, followed closely by a little gingery burp.

Knitbone padded over and put his head in Winnie's lap. In his special doggy way, he knew that something wasn't quite right. He sniffed her hair and cocked his head to one side. Normally Winnie twinkled like sunlight but today she seemed a bit cloudy.

"Are you alright, Winnie?" he asked. "Are you down in the dumps? Do you want to play a game?"

"No, I'm fine, really...actually NO," she suddenly blurted, "NO, I'm NOT fine. It's this daft exhibition business. You were right, Knitbone. It's going to be a disaster. It looks like an explosion in a hat factory down there and Mum and Dad are planning on opening on *Monday*." Winnie gave a hopeless sigh and put her head in her hands. "And not just that. The thing is, I've been on school trips to exhibitions and they don't look anything like Starcross. For a start *they* don't have cobwebs dangling from the ceilings or ivy growing through cracks in the walls. *They* are smart and shiny with guides and shops and everything in the right place. My parents think it's all going to be alright but...oh, you know what they're like!"

The ghosts knew exactly what they were like.

Every generation of Peppers had been properly bonkers. It was a family tradition. There was probably a Pepper crackpot gene.

Knitbone did *not* like the idea of opening Starcross to the public, but he liked the idea of Winnie being sad even less. His ears went flat and he let out a little whimper. All he wanted in the whole world was to make her happy. "Now, now, don't worry, Winnie, we'll help," he woofed, looking at the others. "Won't we, everybody?"

The ghosts smiled at each other. They knew where this was going. Being Beloveds, they were all bound to Starcross by love for their Pepper humans, past and present. So for all of his complaining, the others knew that for Winnie, Knitbone would go to the ends of the earth.

"I didn't think you liked the idea of lots of visitors," teased Valentine, smoothing down his "Gym Bunny" T-shirt.

"Nonsense! I like people!" protested Knitbone,

standing square, his ears up. "In fact, I *love* people!" He thought for a moment and growled a little bit. "Although, come to think of it, I don't like bad people, or hedge hiders, or postmen… Actually I'm not keen on beards either, especially bushy ones that look like squirrels might lurk in them. But, that's not the point." He took a deep breath and said something he suspected he might regret later. "The point is that if Winnie thinks it's a good idea then I *also* think it's a good idea. It's time for an emergency meeting. Dusters at the ready! S.O.S. TO THE RESCUE!"

Chapter 4

DREAM TEAM

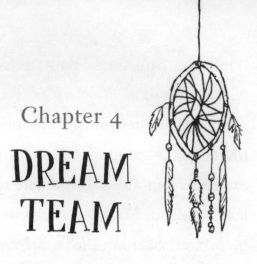

As the clock downstairs chimed ten, Orlando licked a piece of chalk and, on the back of the attic door, wrote:

Snugglers and Spoons

Knitbone gave the little monkey a hard stare, one eyebrow raised quizzically.

Orlando huffed and rubbed it out, replacing it with:

Emergency Meeting

"Thank you very much, Orlando." Knitbone turned to the group. "Now, S.O.S. – Spirits of Starcross – we are gathered here today to talk about the state of the house. As we all know, it's in a terrible mess. Since becoming a ghostly taskforce, keeping tip-top fit, fighting swindlers and the forces of evil, I have to admit that we have let the housework go a bit."

Knitbone ran his paw down the list of jobs on his clipboard. "Let's see, today is…Thursday. Everybody needs a job if we are going to get Starcross ready in time for the opening on Monday. Let me see… Orlando, you are in charge of dusting. With those little hands and that long tail you will be able to swing up and get to the worst of the cobwebs."

The monkey stuck out a pouty bottom lip. "Orlando do spoons. Spoons eez dusty."

Knitbone ignored him and carried on. "After that, please go out to the graveyard and deal with the weeds. It's like a jungle out there – generations of Peppers must be turning in their graves. Gabriel, you can lend a hand, or a beak, whichever is easier. We can't let the general public see them in such a state."

Orlando rolled his eyes and sighed. "Okayyyy, dusty-wusty then weedy-peedy."

Knitbone turned to Martin. "You're going to keep an eye on Lady P's menus and make sure they don't get out of hand. You know, hide some of the more 'unusual' ingredients, like nettles, fungus, donkey milk, etc." Martin clicked his heels and gave a salute.

"Now, we come to the matter of a sign. Every good business needs a good sign." Knitbone looked up from his clipboard. "Does anybody have any ideas for a good slogan?"

Everybody thought very, very hard. In fact,

Martin thought *so* hard he went cross-eyed.

Winnie put a hand up shyly. "How about, *Hats Off to Starcross?*"

The group applauded with great enthusiasm, unanimously agreeing that this was the perfect name. Knitbone gazed at her in goggle-eyed admiration. She was SO clever. "Maybe we could have a shop too," said Winnie, already cheering up. "I could order some things to sell, like T-shirts and posters. Adding a few more things to Dad's shopping list shouldn't be a problem."

"Terrific idea. Well done. Now, we come to the hats. They all need to be put on display." Knitbone cocked his head to one side. "Winnie, how many hats are there? Two hundred? Three hundred?"

"Um...at the last count yesterday, there were eighteen thousand, five hundred and sixty-two."

Knitbone's jaw dropped and his tail drooped. "WHAT? HOW many? *Really?* Oh dear." That was a LOT of hats. He felt the need for a howl.

Gabriel flapped his wings and tried to be positive. "I know, why don't you turn it into a big game of find-and-fetch? You LOVE that."

Knitbone's ears pricked up. It was true, he really DID love to play games.

Winnie nodded. "That's a good idea, we'll just keep playing until the hats are all sorted into groups and hung up neatly." She patted Knitbone on the head and he wagged his tail, keen to get going.

Valentine stretched his long legs and yawned. "What about me?"

"Ah yes, Valentine," woofed Knitbone, checking his list. "You're good at art so you will be in charge of the sign *and* the tickets too. We will need about…ooh, at least five hundred or so. Go like the wind. Chop-chop." Knitbone briskly blew his PE whistle before Valentine could protest.

"Right then, Beloveds, let's get moving! Spirits Of Starcross to the rescue again! For heart and home and all that. No time to lose, we open in four days' time. Meet back here for a progress check at 17:00 hours."

"When's that?" whispered Winnie behind her hand.

"Teatime," answered Martin, as Knitbone blew his whistle loudly. "Ghosts always stop for teatime."

But five o'clock came and went and the ghosts didn't stop. There was simply too much to do and it was much harder than it had sounded.

Valentine found using the scissors very tricky and his colouring kept going over the edges.

Orlando fell off a gravestone into a big patch
of thistles. He shouted lots of rude words that
Gabriel would have told him off for, but luckily
they were in Spanish so nobody understood.
Martin had to hide some nettles in his cheeks and
his head swelled up like a tennis ball.

Winnie and Knitbone thought they had the best deal – they could *never* get tired of playing fetch. But, as it turned out, even Knitbone got fed up with a game that never seemed to end.

The clock struck midnight, and still the Beloveds worked on into the night.

HATS OFF TO

Lord and Lady Pepper had long since gone to bed, tucked under their blankets in their nightcaps, unaware that whilst they lay dreaming about spacefish and polka-dot paint, the family home was being transformed by their daughter and its resident ghosts.

Early the next morning, Winnie was woken up by her parents, bouncing up and down on the end of her bed. "Wake up, Winnie, wake up!" Lord Pepper beamed. "This is the best Friday ever! Something *marvellous* has happened! You won't believe it, but your mother and I have done lots of work *IN OUR SLEEP!*"

Winnie pulled the pillow over her head and yawned. In a muffled voice she said, "It was the ghosts, Dad. I've told you about the ghosts."

"Yes, I know, like I said, it was *us* doing it *in our sleep!* Fancy that!"

Sometimes, it was as if Winnie's parents didn't

hear the *actual* words she said. She had told them about the Beloveds again and again, but they just patted her head and winked at each other, happy and proud that their daughter was SO imaginative.

"Smashing stuff it is, Win!" her father continued. "All the hats are mounted, the rooms are clean, the gardens and graveyard are weed-free, there is a magnificent sign on the front door and a towering pile of tickets. There's even a big box of special Starcross merchandise on the doorstep – T-shirts, balloons, pencils, erasers…who'd have thought we could do all that in our sleep when we never got round to it when we were awake!"

Lady P shook her head in wonder. "And all that time I thought I was just dreaming about spacefish… Remarkable." They gave each other a high-five and went downstairs for breakfast.

Knitbone heard all this from inside the wardrobe in the corner of Winnie's bedroom. He would have been able to hear better if Valentine's

foot hadn't been wedged firmly in his right ear.
He used to have the wardrobe all to himself,
but lately the others had been having sleepovers
in it. It felt very crowded and the floor was
covered in biscuit crumbs. It was time to get up.

Knitbone kicked the door open and they all
fell out in a ghostly heap of yawns. The wardrobe
was the perfect size for a single ghost dog,
but rather compact for a whole gang.

"Did you hear that? Well done, everybody!" said Winnie. "What's left on the list?"

Gabriel the goose stretched his wings. "Advertising," he said, yawning.

Orlando stretched out his tiny fists. "Bartonshire snoozepaper say, 'It pays to advertise'...or was it 'Eat peas and apple pies'? Orlando not so sure now. Night-night." He lay spreadeagled on the floor and dropped off back to sleep again, snoring like a teacup piglet.

Knitbone gave a long, long stretch, from the top of his nose to the tip of his tail, pondering the idea. "That's a good idea. Can't Lord P pay for a lovely big advert in the local snooze...I mean *news*paper? It could have a photo and a phone number so that everyone would know about us. There's lots of money left over from the sale of the Vincent Van Fluff paintings. That surely raised enough cash to last us for ever..."

Later that morning, as Winnie and Lord Pepper sat in the ballroom admiring the impressive display of hats, Winnie thought it would be a good moment to suggest Knitbone's idea. But rather than looking pleased, Lord Pepper looked unexpectedly anxious.

"Ah, yes. That's the thing, Winnie," he wheedled. "Bit of a tricky one that. Tricky, tricky, tricky... No money left, you see." He went to the big piggy bank on the mantelpiece, gave it a shake and out fell a button. "No," he chirped brightly. "All gone. Spent the lot of it on hats."

There was a faint *donk* sound from near the piano as Gabriel fainted.

Winnie gaped at her father. "Are you saying that you have spent ALL OF THE MONEY?" she gasped. "All of the thirty-two million pounds from selling the Vincent Van Fluff paintings? The money that meant we could stay at Starcross Hall for ever? Are you MADDER THAN A BOX OF STOATS?"

"Hats can be quite expensive," said Lord
Pepper in a small voice, twiddling with his
dressing-gown cord. He stared hard at it,
not wanting to meet Winnie's eye. Suddenly,
he gasped, his arm outstretched into the distance.
"Oh my goodness! LOOK OVER THERE!"

Everyone turned around. "Where?"

When they turned back, Lord Pepper
had scarpered.

Chapter 5
GHOST WRITER

After an unsatisfying lunch of periwinkle pasta, Winnie sat down on the bottom step of the stairs and sighed. "So, once again, we are poor. Now we really have to make this work. How are we going to get ourselves known?" She scratched Knitbone's ears absent-mindedly. "No one's going to come if they don't know about it. We have to do something to get ourselves noticed."

Orlando leaped up onto Winnie's head.

He bent over and
looked at her
square between
the eyes.
"Snugglers?"
he grinned.

"Shush,
Orlando,"
muttered Valentine,
"everyone is trying to think."

Knitbone thought very hard. What could they
do? He did a sum in his head:

No money + No visitors =
Sad Peppers
Free publicity + Lots of visitors
=
Happy Peppers

PING! He had an idea. "Do you remember when that man from the paper came and wrote stories about Starcross being haunted? Everyone wanted to read about that, didn't they? Where's that newspaper clipping?"

Winnie dashed up to her bedroom and took it out of her dressing-table drawer.

She raced back downstairs and flopped breathlessly by the gang. "Of course! Brilliant idea! There's more than one way to get noticed. You are a very clever canine – get me the phone, Knitbone!"

Winnie held the receiver and dialled nervously. She took a deep breath and pinched

BARTONSHIRE TIMES

FREE CHEESE FOR EVERY READER! PS-10

SPOOKY STARCROSS SPIRITS HAUNT HORRIFIED HOMEBUYERS!

WHO WOULD BUY A HOUSE LIKE THIS?

her nose with her other hand. The rest of the Beloveds squashed up next to the phone, trying to hear. "Hello, is that Mr Dodger, travel writer for the *Bartonshire Times*?" asked Winnie in her best grown-up telephone voice. "This is Mrs…erm…Mrs Fryingpan… Anyway, you know Starcross Hall? Well, there's strange ghostly goings on there again, mark my words. I think your readers would be very interested so you should definitely get down there quick-smart. Goodbye."

Knitbone gave a cheerful woof. "That should do it!"

The next morning, Mr Dodger, reporter for
the local paper, stood on the doorstep with
a notebook and a camera. Before he had had
a chance to say anything, Lord Pepper – rather
like an overexcitable spaniel with a squeaky toy
– launched straight into his welcoming speech.

"Golly, you're a day or two early but never
mind. WELCOME to *Hats Off to Starcross!* We are
beret pleased to meet you! Hahaha! Do you get
it? It's a joke, you see. Winnie's idea. Clever, isn't
it? Here's a ticket and put this hat on, the tour
starts straight away!" Lord Pepper grabbed the
startled man by the hand and dragged him into
the first room.

"THIS is our room of 'Fluffy Hats'." He
dragged the man into the next room. "And THIS
is our room of 'Frightening Hats'. Over THERE
is our room of 'Hats With Unusual Stains'."
He marched out into the corridor, and set off

at speed. "Come on, dear man, keep up!"

Mr Dodger called after him, "Lord Pepper, I'm not here to see a hat exhibition. I'm from the *Bartonshire Times*. We've had a tip-off that there have been strange goings-on again. Are the ghosts back?" He took out his notepad. "LORD PEPPER?"

But Lord P was gone, leaving only an echo of his voice dribbling down the hallway.

Lady Pepper cheerily poked her head around the kitchen door. "You look like you could do with a cup of tea, Mr Podger. I've got *all sorts* of teas. Oh yes, and a snack of course. I'll be back in a tick."

Finally, Mr Dodger was all alone in the hallway. It was time for the Beloveds to do what they did best. Knitbone blew his PE whistle. "Team S.O.S. – *GO!*"

Valentine began running on the spot, working up a speed until his legs were nothing but a blur.

Then – ZOOM – he was off, whizzing past
Mr Dodger like a bullet.

WHOOSH! "Wassat?" gasped the journalist,
feeling a rushing sensation. WHOOSH!
WHOOSH! He made a grab for his hat, which had
been caught up in an unexpectedly strong gust
of wind.

WHOOSH! By Valentine's second lap of the corridor, the pages of the reporter's notebook had begun to flap and flutter like a moth in a jar.

Orlando swung up and over the banisters, landing neatly on top of the reporter's head and began to lick his ears in an affectionate manner. "Aaarrggh!" Mr Dodger cried, thrashing about as if trying to shake a spider out of his hair. "Urrggh! Wet and disgusting!"

Martin clung to the top of a wobbling hatstand, trying to get his balance. Then he dived onto the floor, followed this up with a commando roll and scampered straight up Mr Dodger's trouser leg. Once inside, he clamped himself onto the journalist's kneecap and tickled it without mercy. "Hahaha… No, stop…hahaha! What the…? That tickles! Gerroff! Gerroff, you horrible spooks!"

Lady Pepper reappeared with a silver tray of refreshments. She was wearing her new apron emblazoned with the Peppers' *Pantry Pirates* logo. "Here you are, Mr Podgy, some lovely refreshing tea." She peered at him anxiously. "And just in time. You look a bit pale, if you don't mind me saying so."

Mr Dodger took the cup and drank it all in one grateful gulp. Lady P folded her arms with satisfaction. "Now, that's better, isn't it? Didn't I tell you?" she said, handing him the tray and wandering back into the kitchen. "There's nothing that a nice mug of my seaweed tea can't fix."

Mr Dodger looked at the biscuits on the tray. They were labelled "Cuttlefish Cookies" and "Monkfish Macaroons". He stared down into the teacup. All that remained at the bottom were strands of slimy seaweed, slowly transforming into the head of a dog... (Little did Mr Dodger know Orlando was artfully rearranging them with his tiny monkey finger.) He shrieked, threw the silver tea tray into the air and made a dash for the door. Jonathon Dodger couldn't get out of there fast enough.

As the door swung closed, Lord Pepper reappeared from a room further down the corridor. "Where's that chap gone?" He looked out of the window to see a figure retreating across the courtyard. "Oh. Is he going already? What a shame. I was just about to show him the 'Funny-smelling Hats'."

The Beloveds clapped each other on the back. Hopefully they had made the right impression.

Chapter 6

THE WORST DAY OUT iN THE WORLD

Bright and early, the Sunday papers fell onto the mat with a thud. "It's here!" Knitbone woofed, his tail wagging as Winnie galloped downstairs, the ghosts hot on her heels. She whipped up the newspaper and skipped into the kitchen where her parents were having breakfast. "Let's see what Mr Dodger's got to say!" Winnie chirped, sweeping the jars of marmalade and teacups to one side. She spread the paper flat on the table and briskly turned to the travel section.

SUNDAY TRAVEL REVIEW

STARCROSS HALL - HATS, HAUNTINGS AND HORRID HORROR! By Jonathon Dodger

If your idea of a good day out is staring at thousands of dusty old hats whilst drinking disgusting potions and fending off evil spirits, then Starcross Hall is the place for you. I, however, won't be going back again. EVER.

Scary, strange and dangerous, their new Hats Off to Starcross exhibition is only for those with strong stomachs (in more ways than one). To start off with, I was bamboozled by a hat-obsessed buffoon before Lady Pepper tried to poison me with weird fishy biscuits. If that wasn't enough, I then became a victim of windy ghosts who spat in my ears, tickled my kneecaps and warded me off with portents of doom.

This definitely has the makings of the worst day out in the world. Take my advice, readers, and give it a miss – kissing slugs is more fun!

"OH NO! OH NO NO NO! How did this happen? Now no one will ever come," wailed Lord Pepper, looking crestfallen as he sat down for breakfast. "And *why* is everyone still going on about ghosts?"

"Because we've *got* ghosts, Dad," Winnie sighed flatly. "I've told you about a hundred times."

"I thought he liked my biscuits," sniffed Lady Pepper.

The Beloveds sat under the table, giving off wafts of peppermint. (It is a fact that ghosts smell of peppermint when embarrassed.)

Orlando banged his head miserably with a teaspoon. "Bad monkeybrain, woof-face, bunnychops and bossygooseyboots. You too, mousie-fattybottom," he muttered.

Martin looked outraged. "I'm NOT a mouse, I'm a hamster!" Tactfully, nobody said anything about the fattybottom bit.

Knitbone sat down next to Winnie's chair, tail drooping and ears flat. "Sorry, Winnie, it was my silly idea. We were trying to be fascinating, not frightening. Now no one will want to visit Starcross and everything's ruined."

Winnie tickled his tummy and whispered, "Don't worry, Knitbone, you were only trying to help. We've been poor before and now we're just poor again. How were we to know that Mr Dodger had no sense of humour? Fancy calling it 'the worst day out in the world'. What a nerve."

For the Peppers, the dream had become a nightmare. Opening Starcross Hall to the public had been a disastrous idea. Once again they were flat broke and back to square one. So much for tomorrow's grand opening day. What a flop!

Sunday plodded by and even their favourite antiques programme couldn't cheer them up. Everybody went to bed early, thoroughly fed up and out of ideas.

Monday morning dawned and the Peppers were all woken by the sound of the doorbell. Riiiinng-riiingg-riiingg!

"Alright, alright," Winnie called, "I'm coming." She squirmed out of bed, pattered down the stairs, and shuffled across the hall floor tiles in her bunny slippers. On the landing the sleepy Beloveds gathered to watch, wondering who it could be at this time. With a yawn, Winnie heaved open the enormous front door.

Brilliant yellow sunshine spilled in, flooding all the dark corners with light. It took a while for her eyes to adjust to the blinding brightness, but after a minute or two, she could make out the heads of people – lots and *lots* of people – *queuing down the driveway!* And, near the hedge, a coach was parked with the words "Sunnyside Up Tours" painted on its side.

"Winnie, what's going on?" mumbled Lord P

as he came down the stairs, pulling on his dressing gown and staggering towards the door. "Who are all these people?" He rubbed his eyes and put on his spectacles. "Can I help you?"

An excited man in a waterproof pushed to the front of the queue and pointed at Lord Pepper. "Look, everybody! It's the bamboozling buffoon!"

A gaggle of teenagers shouted, "Where are the ghosts? We want our knees tickled!"

A lady with a pushchair asked, "Which way to the weird cafe?"

An elderly couple in matching baseball caps announced: "We are here for the worst tourist attraction in the world!"

Flummoxed and amazed, Lord Pepper held the door open wide and a torrent of excitable tourists poured through.

Hats Off to Starcross proved to be a huge hit. Tourists LOVED the sheer awfulness of it. They adored the *Pantry Pirates Cafe*. The menu included delights such as "Earwig Eclairs", "Donkey-Milk Lattes", "Toadstool Trifle" and "Grilled Thing". The bestselling dessert was the "Forget-Me-Not Custard" (once eaten, never forgotten). Lady Pepper very thoughtfully provided bowls for the customers to spit bits into.

Lord Pepper's tour was a hoot. It was supposed to be serious, but instead it was hilariously funny because things kept going wrong. For example, in the "Naughty Hats" room, the Peppers had a fine example of a wizarding hat on display. It was part of a pair. The other hat was kept at an exclusive boarding school and was very wise. However, this one was very naughty and shrieked "BADGER'S BUM!" and "PIG'S KNICKERS!" hysterically at anyone who passed.

Out of embarrassment, Lord Pepper ended up showing off. This led to him getting a gladiator's helmet stuck firmly over his eyes and Lady P having to come to the rescue with some slippy "Banana-skin Butter". The crowd loved it. Lord and Lady Pepper could do no wrong, simply by being their usual, chaotic selves. Finally they had found something they were really, really good at.

Amongst this mad-hatter mayhem, the ghosts were the jewels in the crown. Winnie organized a spooking rota, to ensure that no visitor would be left out. Everybody wanted their fair share of spooking, especially the old ladies, who loved a good scream.

In the cafe, the Beloveds took turns crafting seaweed-tea portraits of themselves in the bottom of teacups. People squealed with delight: "OOOH! I've got an angry goose!" or "Mine's a killer hamster!" The ghosts followed the visitors around, tweaking noses and rummaging in handbags, tickling tummies and whispering in ears.

They scared the pants off everyone and it was lots of fun. By lunchtime of the first day, Knitbone had forgotten that he had ever thought

it was a bad idea.
"Who says you can't
teach an old dog new
tricks?" he woofed,
as he blew
raspberries at
a giggling baby
in a pram.

Every visitor
was invited to try
on any hat they
fancied and have
a complimentary
slide down
the spare stairs'
helter-skelter.
They screamed,
they laughed,
they bought novelty
hats in the gift shop.

The day whizzed by until, finally, the last few stragglers went home, happy and exhausted, clutching balloons that said *I've Got a Positive Hattitude.*

The doors finally shut at 6 p.m. and, after counting the ticket stubs, the joyful Peppers realized that they had sold 658 tickets. Lady Pepper was completely out of "Stinkhorn Sausage Rolls" and "Critter Crumble" and had to go to the kitchen to make more for the next day. Lord Pepper had worn himself out and was draped over the banister like an old coat.

The Beloveds staggered upstairs to Winnie's room and collapsed into the wardrobe.

"Good job we're fighting fit," yawned Valentine.

Knitbone sighed and looked out at Winnie. "Can I sleep on the end of your bed tonight, Winnie?"

"Of course, Knitbone! This is all down to you,

after all. You really are a girl's best friend,
you know. Thank you so much for all your help."

Knitbone bounded over, and Winnie bent
down to give him a big kiss on the head, or a
"pooch smooch" as she called it. As exhausted
as he was, Knitbone wagged his tail. If Winnie
was happy, that was all the reward he needed.
His work was done.

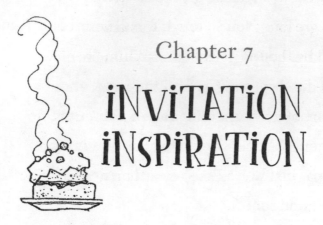

Chapter 7
iNViTATiON iNSPiRATiON

As August rolled on, word got round and soon everybody seemed to have heard of *Hats Off to Starcross*. *The Times* travel section described it as "the best worst tourist attraction in the country", giving it five stars and a thumbs-up. Lord Pepper was interviewed for *Mad Hatter Monthly*. Lady Pepper was asked to appear on Radio 4 to talk about her "Squirty Squid Suppers" and "Lucky Dip Dinners". Her signature dish, "Periwinkle Pasta on a bed of Sea Lettuce", was featured on a television cookery show.

To his great joy, Lord Pepper was quickly contacted by the National Hat Museum of India and invited to host the Eye of Mumbai for three days as part of its world tour. Out of politeness, he offered them the Bristol Bobble Hat in exchange; an item that he had acquired in a charity shop whilst on holiday in the summer of 1976.

Thanks to everyone's efforts and a big dollop of luck, Starcross Hall was busier than it had ever been in all its 904 years. Lord Pepper's dream had finally come true. *Hats Off to Starcross* really was turning out to be the hottest ticket in town.

One morning, whilst the Beloveds were all lying about in Winnie's bedroom, Knitbone was leafing through a pile of old magazines looking for pictures of squirrels, when he came across a brightly-coloured but rather dog-eared advert. A snarling, savage tiger roared out from the page.

Winnie peered over his shoulder. "I've never been to the circus," she said wistfully. "I wonder what it's like?"

Valentine stood up on his hind legs and did a pirouette that turned into a somersault. "It's wonderful, Winnie," he announced. "Full of the fastest, the fittest and the cleverest performers in the world."

Orlando sighed dreamily. "Such lovely snugglers, with shiny fire-sticks."

"Yes," honked Gabriel. "In the old days, whenever Starcross needed a showstopper, the circus was just the ticket!"

Winnie leaped up suddenly. "Well, why don't we do exactly that? We could invite this –" she read the advert – "this *Circus Tombellini* to Starcross! It'll be just like the olden days! The visitors will love it."

She ferreted around in her dressing-table drawer, found a stationery set and a pen and began to scribble away.

"But we don't know the address," protested Knitbone, inspecting the date of the advert. "And this magazine is at least fifty years old!"

Winnie popped the letter into an envelope and licked it shut. On the front she had written:

Circus Tombellini
The Greatest Show on Earth

"Will it get there?" asked Knitbone doubtfully. "The address is a bit vague."

Winnie looked at him thoughtfully. "Well, it works for messages in bottles. Fingers crossed."

She stuck a stamp on it, dropped it in the postbox during the Beloveds' morning run, and hoped for the best.

A week later a postcard landed *plop* on the Starcross doormat. On the front was an old-fashioned photograph of a boy and a tiger.

Winnie turned it over. On the back it simply said:

Thank you for your kind invitation.
See you on Saturday.
Alberto Tombellini (Ringmaster)

Winnie made the big announcement over dinner and everyone cheered. Lord Pepper put on his celebratory crown and Lady Pepper set about planning a special Circus Menu. Valentine

ran circuits around the kitchen and Gabriel
flapped and honked.

Martin
did some
laps in
the salad
spinner
and Orlando
was so
overcome with joy
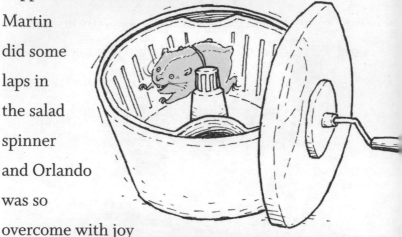
that he had to be put to bed early, clasping
a bunch of soothing teaspoons.

Knitbone, however, was rather quiet.
Sniffing Alberto Tombellini's postcard carefully,
he couldn't help noticing that it had an odd
perfume. It smelled of sawdust, popcorn and
a third...*something*, something that he couldn't
quite put his paw on. It made him feel
uncomfortable and a whimper came up like
a hiccup.

"Are you alright, Knitbone?" asked Winnie, breaking off from the celebrations.

"Oh, yes! Perfectly!" He wiggled his bottom so that it looked like he was wagging his tail. "See?"

Winnie was so happy, that Knitbone just hoped he'd got the wrong end of the stick.

Chapter 8

CIRCUS SURPRISE

Circus Tombellini arrived out of nowhere, in the middle of the night. No one heard them arrive. No one heard them pitch the tent. It was almost as if the circus had flown there, or emerged from the morning mist like a velvety mushroom.

It was a thing of beauty. A towering canvas tent of dreams. Draped in thick stripes of butter yellow and strawberry scarlet, it was topped with fluttering flags. The doors were as blue as a deep ocean, embroidered with silver stars and edged with sparkling gold braid. The guy ropes were decorated with dancing rainbow bunting. Circus Tombellini's Big Top was a truly magnificent affair.

The Beloveds pressed beaks, faces and noses against the attic window, pushing and shoving each other to get a better look. There were lots of accompanying "oooh"s and "aahhh"s.

"It looks so exciting," gasped Martin.

"Maybe there will be snugglers!" exclaimed Orlando. "Let's go down and see."

Just as they turned to leave, Knitbone caught sight of something moving in the doorway of the tent. His hackles went up and his doggy senses began to tingle. Knitbone Pepper found himself in a Big Bark Situation.

"WOOF! WOOF WOOF!"

"Wassup, Woof-face?" asked Orlando. "You see a squizzel?"

"There's something there, right *there*, in the doorway of the tent. I saw it," Knitbone growled, nose pressed firmly against the window, tail pointing straight up and quivering.

"Well, yes, dear boy," said Valentine, smoothing out his long ears. "It's a circus. There will be all sorts inside. Come on, I want to see if there are acrobats."

"Yes, come on, Knitbone, let's go!" said Gabriel, flapping his wings.

Knitbone got down from the window, tucking his growl back into his chest.

Martin patted his paw. "'S alright, you daft thing, you're just overreacting. You can't help it, you're a dog, it's just what you do. All your lot are like it. Now, let's go and have some fun!"

Lord Pepper was already on the lawn greeting his new guests. He had chosen to wear a Roman centurian's helmet because it was a special occasion. Lady P was wearing a silk evening gown, having created a breakfast tureen of Circus Soup in their honour, which she was currently sloshing all over the lawn.

An elderly man dressed in a long, red coat with shiny brass buttons stepped forward. He held out a gloved hand, which Lord Pepper grasped and began pumping up and down like a handle.

"*Buongiorno, buongiorno!* My name is Alberto Tombellini," the man announced, "and I am the Ringmaster of Circus Tombellini. It is our great honour to perform in the grounds of Starcross Hall."

Lord Pepper glowed with happiness. "My dear fellow, what a *delight* to meet you! Fancy the circus actually coming to Starcross – my ancestors would have been thrilled! I am Lord Hector Pepper and this is my wife, Lady Isadora."

"Ah, the lovely Isadora," said Alberto in his Italian accent, bowing low and kissing her hand.

"Chef fantastico. A great pleasure to meet you, *bella signora*."

Lady P was speechless with excitement, so she just blushed and tried not to spill pink soup down her front.

Lord Pepper put a proud arm around his wife. "Can I introduce you to our daughter, Lady Winifred Clementine Violet Araminta Pepper? She's simply splendid." He gestured towards

Winnie, puffing out his chest.

"*Daaaad!*" cringed Winnie. She stepped
forward and held out her hand. "Nice to meet
you, Mr Tombellini, but everyone just calls
me Winnie."

Alberto gave her hand a firm shake and winked. "Ah, Winnie Pepper, so clever of you to find us at the right address. Thank you for inviting us. All my friends call me Bertie and I think – no, I *know* – that we will be friends."

His face was as round and shiny as a rosy apple. A sleek silver moustache perched on his upper lip, curly with swirls on the end. Alberto Tombellini's face seemed kind and warm, but Winnie couldn't help noticing that his dark brown eyes were rather sad.

Suddenly Bertie clapped his hands, breaking the spell and making everyone jump. "Circus Soup! How lucky we are. I always say that there is nothing quite like pink soup for breakfast. Goodness, floating bits of hot dogs and candyfloss? How inventive, although I would like to save mine for later if you do not mind. Do come in and meet the rest of the troupe." He waved them all into the tent.

"What do you think?" Winnie whispered to Knitbone, who had appeared by her side.

"I think there's more to him than meets the eye," said Knitbone, sniffing the air.

"My thoughts exactly," muttered Winnie as they stepped inside.

What Knitbone *didn't* say as he trotted at Winnie's heel, was that he had figured out what the third mystery smell on the postcard was.

Chapter 9

SNUGGLERS AND SECRETS

Knitbone was very good at smelling smells. People didn't realize that feelings had their own perfume, because it was a dog secret. For example, happy people smelled of warm buttered toast, whilst grumpy people smelled of rusty nails and mud.

Knitbone had only smelled a broken heart once before, and that had been Winnie's. She had smelled like that for ages after he had died: an odd mixture of salt, mist and dandelion clocks, of empty drawers, fallen leaves and the faintest shadowy scent of violets. Bertie Tombellini smelled just like that and so did his postcard.

It hurt Knitbone to think about it. It made his tail droop and his ears go flat. Something was wrong. Knitbone did not like this, so he tried concentrating on the tent instead.

Peculiarly, the inside of the tent seemed a lot bigger than the outside. The ghosts made themselves at home, stretching out on the tiered wooden seats that ran around the edge. In the middle was a large arena, filled with light and sawdust.

Martin nudged Orlando. "Look! It's that flaky stuff that I used to have in my cage. Gets stuck in your teeth. Doesn't fill you up either."

But Orlando was already up and off, swinging from the trapeze, singing rude sea shanties at the top of his voice.

Unaware of these ghostly gymnastics, Bertie began to introduce his troupe to the Peppers.

"This is Mario, our Strongman." A mountain
of a man stepped forward. He had one enormous
arm around a tiny, red-haired woman who was,

in turn, holding a sweet dimpled baby in the
crook of her arm. "And this is Evangelina, our
remarkable fire-eater." The tiny woman curtsied
as her baby giggled and wriggled in her arms.

He was wearing a red Babygro with *Tombellini Toddler* embroidered on the front in sequins. Bertie smiled indulgently at the baby. "Here we have their son, the Astounding Aldo. We don't know what Aldo is going to be yet but we know absolutely that whatever it is, it will be astounding."

Bertie pointed at a group of ten performers, all dressed in sparkly leotards. "These are four generations of Tombellinis. They are tumblers, trampolinists, tightrope walkers and trapeze artists. They are also talented musicians." The group lined up with their assortment of instruments, white teeth gleaming, and waving in perfect time. The Peppers grinned and waved back like chaotic chimps.

Bertie turned to his left, where a tall man in a star-covered cloak stood. "This is the Amazing Umbonzo. He is a master illusionist and magician." As Umbonzo leaned forwards

to shake hands, a blizzard of streamers flew out
of his cloak.

"Oops," he smiled.
"That's always
happening!"

As the Peppers watched the ribbons drift away, a loud parping came from the back of the tent. A tiny car pulled up and three clowns got out, offering jumbo-sized white-gloved hands to their hosts. "Hello, Peppers! We are Bish, Bash and Bosh. Nice to meet you."

Lord Pepper grasped Bosh's hand and was promptly given an electric shock. *BUZZZZZZZ!* The clowns rolled about on the floor laughing and squishing custard pies into each other's faces.

Bertie sighed apologetically. "I'm afraid clowns have terrible manners. So," he looked around, "I think that's everybody...except for the jugglers. They should be here by now, but they always take ages in the supermarket as they can't just put the vegetables in the trolley like everyone else."

Orlando squealed, "Hooray for SNUGGLERS!" from the rafters.

Winnie stepped forwards. "Hang on a minute," she said, remembering the advert and the postcard that Bertie had sent them. "Don't you have a tiger?"

Cheerful bright Bertie seemed to shrink a little and looked down at his boots with a small frown. "Tiger? No, no, Winnie Pepper, I am afraid you are very much mistaken. There are definitely no animals at Circus Tombellini, only people. Now I'm afraid you must excuse me, so much to do."

He took a twinkling gold watch out from his waistcoat pocket and snapped it open and shut. "There's always less time than you think."

As Bertie stepped out of the blue circus door and retreated into his trailer, the sharp scent of heartbreak was almost too much for Knitbone to bear.

Chapter 10

DOGGY DETECTIVE

The day had got off to an excellent start, and plans swung into action. Winnie pinned posters to the iron gates. They said:

HATS OFF TO
CIRCUS TOMBELLINI!
FOR TWO NIGHTS ONLY
THE CIRCUS
WILL BE AT
STARCROSS HALL,
BOOK NOW FOR
**THE GREATEST SHOW
ON EARTH**

Whilst all the other ghosts were busy with the "daily spook" (tickling and terrifying tourists, whispering words like "Big Top" and "Book now!" in unsuspecting ears), Knitbone snuck out for a bit of a sniff around the shadows in the circus tent. He still couldn't shake the itchy feeling that something wasn't *quite* right.

He nosed his way underneath the gold braid of the tent door and sat on one of the wooden benches. It was very quiet except for a lone juggler, practising with three carrots, an onion and a cabbage. Knitbone thought he would take the weight off his paws and watch for a while.

As a ghost, Knitbone couldn't be seen by normal people, so he could watch the juggling undisturbed and pretend it was all for him. He really loved watching things being thrown.

After some impressive hurling, the juggler put down his vegetables and picked up some fire-sticks. Knitbone's ears pricked up, sticks were even better than cabbages!

The man lit the sticks and tossed them into the air. They spun and twirled like sparkling fireworks. The best bit was when he managed to balance one on the tip of his chin. Even Knitbone, who considered himself something of a stick expert, couldn't do that. *Brilliant!* he thought, woofing and wagging his tail in appreciation. "Bravo!"

Knitbone was enjoying the show so much that he almost didn't notice the shape lurking in the shadows. It was only when the flames from the fire-sticks cast a flash of light against the

back of the tent that Knitbone saw something which made his fur prickle.

Knitbone's ears flattened and he stood up slowly. A low growl escaped from his lips as he slid off the bench and backed towards the exit. All of his animal instincts told him that there was a Bad Thing in the circus tent.

"WINNIE! WINNIE! WINNIE!" Knitbone barked, bursting out into the sunshine and bounding over the lawn. He galloped across the gravel, up the stone steps and skidded to a halt in the hallway. "WINNIE!" he howled at the top of his voice. "STAY AWAY FROM THE CIRCUS!"

Winnie appeared from the kitchen looking perplexed, and ushered Knitbone into the coat cupboard, out of the exhibition visitors' earshot, pulling the door to.

"What on earth is wrong, you loopy dog?" she asked, switching on the cupboard light. "The whole point of the circus is that you

DON'T stay away from it. Roll up, roll up, and all that."

"Yes, what's the matter?" yawned Martin, poking his head out of the top of a wellington boot. Since Starcross Hall had opened to the public, the coat cupboard had become the Beloveds' unofficial staffroom, as the attic was just too far away. It was permanently stocked with energy-giving ginger biscuits and special places for napping. Unsurprisingly Martin was in there a lot.

"I was just taking a nap before my turn on the knee-tickler shift. I think I'm supposed to be nocturnal...or is the word numerical? I might be electrical. Maybe it's eternal." He stretched out one of his little arms, followed by the other. "Whatever the word is, I do love a nice afternoon nap."

"Never mind that!" Knitbone took a deep breath and tried to calm down, but his eyes were wide with horror. "Listen...there's a BAD THING on the loose out there, wandering about, ready to attack AT ANY MOMENT!" He knew that this was probably a bit of an exaggeration, but he was already getting swept up in the drama.

Winnie, who had settled down on a small stool, stroked his ears and smiled. "Are you sure, Knitbone? Do you remember that visitor's suitcase that you thought was full of squirrels?"

Martin chipped in, "And the scarf that you said had angry patterns?"

Gabriel nudged open the cupboard door and poked his beak round. "And the teapot that looked at you in a funny way?"

"No, this is different – although that teapot was definitely dodgy – this is serious!"

"Wassup with woof-face?" asked Orlando, swinging through the doorway and landing neatly on the hatstand.

"Knitbone thinks there's a Bad Thing on the loose and it's very dangerous," smiled Winnie.

"Ooh, like when he say that clouds are 'savage fluff'?" grinned Orlando.

Valentine bounded in from the corridor.

"Or like when he was scared of the washing machine?"

"NO, NO, *NO!* Not like that AT ALL!" Knitbone frowned. "Listen, I have seen *something* in the tent and you –" he prodded his nose at Winnie – "*you* are not to go in there under any circumstances. Do you hear me, young lady?"

It took exactly two and a half seconds before everyone had piled out of the cupboard, and was running towards the circus tent with Knitbone howling in hot pursuit.

By the time they got there, the juggler had
gone. The circus tent was just a big, echoey cave
full of drifting motes of dust sparkling in a shaft
of sunlight. Everything was very still, as if the
tent had fallen asleep.

The Beloveds and Winnie crept very quietly round the arena, looking carefully under benches and behind poles for any evidence of the Bad Thing. But there was nothing.

They were about to tell Knitbone that he was bonkers, when a low, quiet growl rolled out of the shadows. They all stopped dead in their tracks. Orlando squeaked and leaped into Winnie's arms.

"YOU SEE?" hissed Knitbone, eyebrows raised to the ceiling. "There! Didn't I tell you? Now let's *go!*"

Orlando clamped himself on top of Winnie's head and began to whimper. "Orlando know this sound. He hear it in olden days. No doubt."

"WHAT *IS* IT?" whispered everyone together.

"Eez big, huge, massive, spiky snaggletooth. Tut tut. Oh noes. Is very bad." He covered his ears with Winnie's plaits. "Now everyone's a-gonna die, except for the dead ones, that is," he added helpfully, "'cos they is dedders already."

"WHAT? A *spiky snaggletooth*?" Winnie's heart pounded and her eyes were as big as saucers. "Whatever it is, we need to raise the alarm!" They made a dash for the door when another deeper, darker rumble rolled around the tent like thunder.

Slowly, out of the shadows, padded the biggest tiger Winnie had ever seen: a riot of fiery oranges and snowy whites. He had a white flash on his nose in the shape of a star, his round eyes glowed like yellow moons and his teeth shone like icicles.

Winnie and Knitbone shot a glance at each other. They would have recognized this creature anywhere – it was the tiger from the old magazine advert! For a moment, Winnie forgot how to breathe.

The tiger circled the group, not taking his steady luminous eyes off them for a second,

panting and pacing. His whiskers twitched
and he licked his nose with a wet pink tongue
the size of a table mat. Valentine, Gabriel
and Martin immediately played dead, whilst
Orlando dived head first into Winnie's pocket.
(For dead animals, they had surprisingly
strong survival instincts.)

A scream stuck in Winnie's throat, lodged there like a big toffee. Terrified, she realized that she couldn't make a sound. She trembled like a jelly and waited for the worst.

Undeterred, Knitbone leaped to the rescue. This was the most important Big Bark Situation he had ever been in. He sprang in between Winnie and the tiger, fur up on end, growling and snarling for all he was worth. "Get away! Get away, you big…big…MOGGY! Don't you DARE touch her! You'll be sorry if you so much as lay a paw on Winnie!" he barked.

But the tiger didn't pounce or swipe or bite.

Instead, he gave a big sad sigh, dropped down onto one furry knee and lowered his enormous head. "I'm very sorry I've frightened you. I can't help it. Everything I say sounds growly. I didn't think anyone could hear me. Please don't tell anybody, I don't want to get in trouble." The air suddenly filled with the scent of peppermint.

Orlando popped his head out of Winnie's pocket and clapped his little hands in delight. "Of COURSE, big spiky snaggletooth is a *ghost*!"

Chapter 11

LETTiNG THE CAT OUT OF THE BAG

The tiger stood up. He was the size of a car (and a big one at that) and he loomed over them all like a stripy thundercloud. On closer inspection, they could see that he was definitely wispy around the edges. Everyone calmed down and began to relax.

"Who *are* you?" growled Knitbone suspiciously.

"My name is the Mighty Rajah. But you can call me Roojoo."

Martin stepped forward and skewered a ginger biscuit on the end of his sword. "Would you like one of these? You look like you could do with one."

Roojoo accepted the biscuit gratefully. "Thank you. These are my favourites. How did you know?"

"Wild guess," muttered Martin, rolling his eyes.

Knitbone still didn't trust the tiger. "Why don't you want Winnie to tell anybody about you?"

"Well," munched Roojoo, "I don't think I'm supposed to be here."

"You can say that again," honked Gabriel. "Bertie said that his circus only has human people in it."

Roojoo stopped eating his biscuit and gave a deep sigh. "I know."

"Hang on a minute," said Valentine. "Are you just a ghost, or are you –" he gave a heavy wink – "a *special* ghost?"

Roojoo looked perplexed.

Orlando inspected the tiger's whiskers one by one. "What bunnychops mean is – *is you Beloved*?"

Roojoo blinked his big eyes. "What is 'beloved'?"

"*We* is Beloveds, you silly sausage!" squealed Orlando.

Winnie explained, "A Beloved is a ghost

animal who is so devoted to their special person that they wait for them for ever. Knitbone here is *my* Beloved." She stroked Knitbone's silky ears. Knitbone growled again and glared at the tiger, just to make a point. "Actually, I'm surprised I can see you," continued Winnie, scratching her head. "I thought I could only see Pepper Beloveds."

Roojoo sighed. "My special person hasn't noticed me for a very, very long time." A single tear trickled down his nose and plopped into the sawdust.

"Poor lonely snaggletooth," crooned Orlando, patting the tiger's fur kindly with his tiny pink hand. "But who *is* your special person?"

Winnie and Knitbone looked at each other, remembering the photograph of the boy and his tiger on the old-fashioned postcard.

Roojoo gave another deep, sad sigh. "Can't you guess?"

Chapter 12

ROLL UP! ROLL UP!

That evening, the queue outside the circus tent was very long. Visitors had spent all day looking at the hats, eating strange things and being tickled by ghosts. Finishing off the day at the circus was the perfect end to a perfectly peculiar day at Starcross. They clutched their tickets and chattered like excited sparrows.

From inside the big house came a series of loud bangs, followed by a crash and a whimper. After a hard day's work, Lord Pepper was practising tobogganing down the stairs on a silver tea tray.

"I'm so excited – opening night for Circus Tombellini tonight and the Eye of Mumbai arrives first thing tomorrow morning. I'm the luckiest lord in the land! Are you read-d-d-d-dy, dear?" he cried, bumping down the last few steps. He was wearing a wizard's hat and cloak, all set for the evening ahead.

"Oh yes!" declared Lady Pepper, emerging from the kitchen and patting her hair with floury hands. "I've made some spicy 'Volcano Popcorn' for the performance. It tasted a bit tame so I added thirty-four red-hot chillis and a flowerpot full of mustard. Best be careful or you'll become a fire-eater too, haha!" She grabbed a tiara from a nearby display and popped it on. "Pepper by name, pepper by nature. Come on, Hector!"

Lord and Lady P pushed their way to the front of the queue, stepping over picnic baskets and handbags. "Excuse me, yes, thank you, excuse me, Peppers coming through..." Winnie trailed behind, feeling embarrassed.

"Welcome to our circus," said Roojoo with pride as Winnie and the Beloveds entered the tent. He nodded his huge head at a space in the wings of the arena. "You'll get the best view from there, so make yourself at home.

Now if you'll excuse me, I have to do my warm-up."

"Warm-up?" asked Valentine. "I hope you haven't forgotten, but you are dead. Why do you need to do a warm-up?"

"You'll see," said Roojoo, winking one big, golden eye. "I still like to play my part. People used to say, 'Have you seen the Bengal tiger they call Rajah? He's so frightening!' I was rather famous in my day and I like to keep my paw in, deceased or not. One never knows when one might be needed. It's important to keep fit."

Soon the queue had trailed in, and everyone was seated, waiting for the spectacle to unfold. The air tingled with excitement, laced with a delicious scent of popcorn and candyfloss. Sparkling silvery ropes and hoops hung from the ceiling and as the lights went down, waterfalls of spotlights lit up the central arena as an acrobat with a golden trumpet played a fanfare. Bertie, resplendent in a red glittery coat, grey gloves and top hat, greeted the crowd with a deep bow.

"Ladies and gentlemen, children of all ages – welcome to Circus Tombellini, courtesy of Starcross Hall!" The spotlight swung onto Lord and Lady Pepper, who were sitting in the front row, stuffing their faces with popcorn. Lord Pepper looked both thrilled and alarmed, whilst his wife's face was the colour of a tomato. "Tonight you will witness the incredible, the remarkable, and the downright amazing!" The crowd clapped and stamped their feet. "So now, without further ado, it is my pride and pleasure to introduce to you the first act of the evening… The legendary fire-breather – Evangelina Blaze!"

A woman cartwheeled into the ring to thunderous applause and flashing cameras. The little red-haired mother they had met earlier in the day was not as the Beloveds remembered her.

Somehow, she had transformed into a fabulous
fairy-tale creature, with stars in her hair and
rainbow ribbons streaming from her costume.
She wore a dragon mask and when
she flapped her wings a torrent of
fire poured out of her mouth.

"WOW! Look
at THAT!"
exclaimed Winnie,
clapping hard.

Over the next hour the
crowd gasped at the high-wire acts and guffawed
at the clowns. They cheered as Mario the
Strongman was fired from a glitter cannon and
whooped as the Amazing Umbonzo somehow
managed to make a bicycle disappear into thin air.

During the interval Lady Pepper ate too much Volcano Popcorn and had to be hosed down by the clowns, which was very entertaining in itself and resulted in an appreciative round of applause from the audience.

Then the lights went down again as one of the acrobats picked up his violin and began to play. The beautiful music rose as the jugglers skipped into the ring, swinging their clubs and hoops, much to Orlando's delight. All eyes were on the jugglers as they began to toss six, seven, eight objects into the air.

All eyes, that is, except for those of Winnie and the Beloveds, watching from the wings. Because unbeknownst to the cheering crowd, the Mighty Rajah had entered the ring.

The ghost tiger prowled around the arena, a low growl escaping from his jaws. In graceful silence, he jumped up onto a stool and stood on his back legs, stretching up to the ceiling with

perfect balance. Winnie looked
around in case anyone else had noticed,
but the audience's attention was firmly fixed on
the jugglers. Like all the other ghosts, Roojoo
was completely invisible to everyone but Winnie.

Ready for the finale of the jugglers' act, three
standing hoops of fire burned around the ring.
Roojoo leaped through each of them in turn,
pouncing and bouncing and swooping and

soaring to the strains of
the cello, like a big orange bird.
He seemed to glide through the air as if he
were flying. The tiger balanced on one paw,
then another, spinning like a ballerina before
launching into a triple somersault in the air and
landing sure-footed like the graceful big cat he
was. Finally, he let out an enormous roar that
made Winnie's eyes water.

Winnie and the ghosts gave a big cheer (which was a bit embarrassing as the jugglers hadn't even finished. Winnie had to turn it into a coughing fit so nobody noticed).

Roojoo bowed to his audience of six, lowering his big head to the floor, his stripy tail whipping back and forth. Orlando gave a whoop and Gabriel stamped his feet. "Yeah, Roojoo! What a star! Way to go! Bravo! Encore!"

Roojoo looked over at the doorway of the tent, where Bertie stood, gazing down at his pocket watch, completely unaware that his Beloved was so close.

"Poor Roojoo," whispered Knitbone. "I wish we could help."

"Yes," sighed Valentine, who still thought about his own Pepper person every day. "Being a Beloved can be dead lonely."

Chapter 13

A BELOVED iN NEED IS A FRIEND iNDEED

At bedtime, even though it had been a very exciting evening, Roojoo's situation was the main topic of conversation. The exhausted Beloveds sat on the end of Winnie's quilt and tried to think of what they could do to help. It didn't seem fair that they all had each other and Roojoo was alone. They realized how lucky they were.

"Can't we just tell Bertie?" asked Winnie. "I would have loved it if somebody had told me that Knitbone was still around."

The Beloveds looked at each other doubtfully. Knitbone cocked his right ear and raised an eyebrow. "Would you have believed I was here unless you'd seen me with your own eyes?"

Winnie sighed and shrugged. She knew the answer.

Valentine scratched his ear with his back foot. "It's a tricky area because even after all this time it's a complete mystery how it all works. Do you remember the page that was ripped out of *The Good Ghost Guide*? Page 84?"

"A page? What page? I didn't know there was a page! There are instructions that tell you how to reunite a Beloved with their special person?" Winnie jumped up. "Why didn't we think of this before? Where is it?"

"Hold your horses," woofed Knitbone. "We have no idea *where* that page could be, or who tore it out. You and I just got lucky. Let's not get Roojoo's hopes up."

Crestfallen, Winnie sat back down with a thump.

"Couldn't we just cheer Roojoo up until he has to leave again?" asked Martin. "He doesn't seem to know much about being a Beloved. We could put on a quiz or do some dancing..."

"We could tell him a thing or two about being a ghost?" suggested Gabriel. "You know, put on a few history classes or something involving lots of lovely books. Oooh! We could call it Spooky School!"

"Hmmm," said Knitbone doubtfully. "He strikes me as more of an action tiger than a book lover. We could certainly show him *The Good Ghost Guide* though, that might be useful..." Suddenly his tail drooped again. "Oh, hang on a minute. The book is in the library and Roojoo has to stay in the tent."

Winnie looked confused, so Gabriel explained. "Rule number 2 of the Handy Hints and Tips in the Guide. *A Beloved is tied to their home for ever.* So, wherever the tent goes, Roojoo can go too. But even though the circus can go from Brazil to Bangladesh, Roojoo is bound to the tent because it's the place that he and Bertie call home. I bet he's the best travelled stay-at-home spook you could hope to meet!"

"Beloveds wait at home and hope we get finded all over again," explained Orlando.

Valentine went on, "Pepper Beloveds have always had the run of the house and the grounds, right up to the Estate bus stop, so we are very lucky. As the whole Starcross Estate has been home to the Peppers for centuries, our hauntings are what you might call 'roomy'."

Knitbone stretched from head to tail and gave a big yawn. "There's nothing to stop us taking the book to him though, is there? He's only here for one more day. Remember: 'a Beloved in need is a friend indeed'."

Knitbone crossed over to Winnie's window and looked out across the courtyard to the lawn. The tent stood silent in the moonlight. Through the open doorway, he could just make out a huge shadowy shape, waving a giant paw, as if to say "Goodnight".

Chapter 14

THE STARCROSS SPARKLER

"Today is the day!" announced Lord Pepper the next morning, stuffing a kipper in his pocket and scoffing a triangle of toast. "The Eye of Mumbai will be here at ten."

"The Sigh of Moon-pie?" murmured Lady Pepper, sipping her radish smoothie.

"No, the EYE of MUMBAI, dear. You know, like the place in India." Lord Pepper slid his (now rather battered) copy of *Mad Hatter Monthly* down the table to where Winnie sat, pouring milk onto her cereal.

It was open on an article with lots of photos. There were brightly painted elephants on parade, garlands of yellow flowers and pretty ladies in colourful silk saris. The biggest photo was in black and white, featuring a man in a turban sitting on a throne, brandishing a big curved sword. He looked very important. On his head he was wearing a magnificent turban, draped with row upon row of pearls. In the centre of the turban sat a massive glittering ruby.

"That's the Maharajah, who is rather like a king," said Lord Pepper. "And that," he pointed his toast corner at a modern coloured photo of the large, glittering brooch, "is the Eye of Mumbai today."

The blood-red ruby sent out shafts of crimson light. But despite its beauty, there was something very peculiar about it. It wasn't even the shape of an eye, but for some reason it definitely seemed to look at you. It was starey and rather glarey.

"That looks like it's worth a penny or two," said Lady Pepper, drying up a jug and peering over Winnie's shoulder.

Lord Pepper waved his hand dismissively, spattering his dressing gown with bits of parsnip marmalade. "Maybe a few million trillion squidoodles… whatever. The point *is* that the Eye of Mumbai is the most remarkable piece of headwear jewellery in the world and it's coming to Starcross Hall today!"

"But that's a fortune!" spluttered Winnie. "How will we keep it safe?"

"Well, I *will* be lending them our Bobble Hat of Bristol in exchange," huffed Lord Pepper. "It is genuine alpaca wool, you know…it's very valuable. Well, it is to me. Anyway, the nice man from the National Hat Museum of India asked all about our security arrangements and he said that our situation was ideal."

"But we don't HAVE any security arrangements," protested Winnie. "We don't even lock the front door. Your idea of security is holding your trousers up with string!"

Her father looked down at his droopy pyjama bottoms and frowned.

Knitbone nudged Winnie's knee with his wet nose. "Never mind about all that, Winnie Pepper. One thing at a time. *We've got tigers to teach.* Come on."

Chapter 15

TEACHER'S PET

Winnie lugged *The Good Ghost Guide* over to the circus tent. "It's heavier than it looks," she puffed.

"That's the extra-large ideas," explained Gabriel. "In order to fit them onto the pages, they get squashed up, so the book weighs a lot."

"You're back! Good morning, everyone," said Roojoo, greeting Winnie and the Beloveds at the door of the tent, his eyes shining with excitement.

"Morning, Roojoo," they chorused.

Roojoo peered at the book which Winnie had placed in the middle of the arena. Little specks of sawdust rose up in the morning light. Except for them, the tent was quite empty.

"What is that you have there?"

Gabriel flapped his white wings and gave a honk. "This is *The Good Ghost Guide*, full of marvellous hints and tips for ghosts."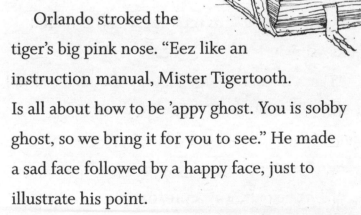

Orlando stroked the tiger's big pink nose. "Eez like an instruction manual, Mister Tigertooth. Is all about how to be 'appy ghost. You is sobby ghost, so we bring it for you to see." He made a sad face followed by a happy face, just to illustrate his point.

"For me? Really? How kind. It's been a very long time since I had anyone to help me. I don't know what to say." Roojoo gave a big sniff and Orlando had to hold on to Winnie so as not to get sucked up his enormous nose. "There is just one thing, though."

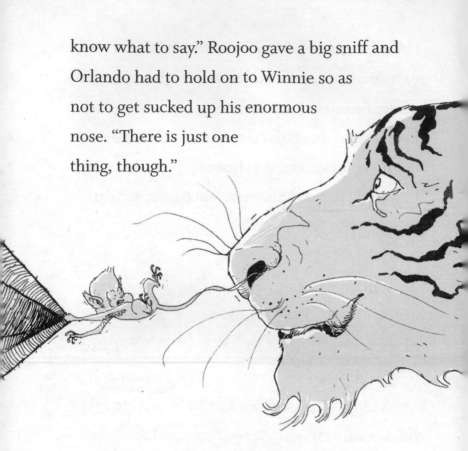

The tiger shook his big head and looked embarrassed. "I'm afraid I'm not a very good reader. I prefer being read *to*, you see."

"Don't be daft, we can read it to you," woofed Knitbone. "What are friends for?"

Roojoo looked up in surprise. "We are *friends*?

How wonderful. When you are a tiger, it's not easy to make friends. I don't know why." He gave a big grin, showing two rows of huge white teeth.

Everybody felt a bit nervous but had the good manners not to show it. Instead they all sat down in a cosy corner of the tent and began to turn the pages.

The book was very informative, full of interesting chapters and articles. They chose a chapter called "Cheering Tunes for the Downhearted". This was a list of songs suggested for ghosts in need of a bit of a boost, such as "All Things Bright and Beautiful", "You are my Sunshine" and "If You're Happy and You Know It Clap Your Wings/Paws/Flippers". They had a loud, morale-boosting singalong and then settled down for a biscuit break.

"The thing is, Knitbone Pepper," said Roojoo, munching away, "I can't help noticing that your special person," he nodded at Winnie, "is very much alive, just like my Bertie. This fills my heart with hope. For fifty years, I have waited, hoping that one day Bertie might notice me by his side, but to no avail. It is my greatest sadness, for I love him more than anything in the whole world. I am longing to know – how is it you became reunited?"

Knitbone looked at Winnie, Winnie looked at Gabriel, Gabriel looked at Valentine and Valentine looked at Orlando. Orlando would have looked at Martin but unfortunately Martin had got his head stuck in a nearby popcorn carton.

The truth was that nobody knew the answer and they didn't understand why Winnie could see them either.

"I'm sorry, Roojoo," said Winnie. "It's a bit of a blur. I'm not exactly sure how it happened – it just did." Winnie struggled to remember. "I was very sad for a long time and then one day... there he was. It's all a bit hazy, I'm afraid." She gave Knitbone a hug.

Gabriel rested his beak on Roojoo's shoulder. "Without the right instructions, it's just down to guesswork."

"Page 84 would have had the answer, I suppose," mumbled Martin from inside the carton, before anyone could stop him. "Such a shame that it's missing from the book."

Roojoo let out a heart-rending roar. "Missing? But wheeeeerrrrre has it gone? It's my only chance. Can't you find it? I need it!"

Helpless, Knitbone whimpered, "We don't know where it is, I looked everywhere for it... look!" Knitbone opened *The Good Ghost Guide* and turned the pages to 81, 82...but there was just a torn edge where page 84 should have been. "I'm so sorry, Roojoo."

The tiger's huge orange shoulders slumped in disappointment.

"It's not just you. We've all had to get used to the idea," said Valentine in a quiet voice. "Knitbone and Winnie are very lucky to be reunited. In fact it's the first time I've seen it happen in the whole of my 823 years."

"Eez best if you can keep busy as a bee,"
mumbled Orlando, wiping a tear away.

"Friends help." Gabriel draped a heartfelt
wing across Roojoo's back.

"But I'm only here for one more night,"
wailed Roojoo. "Then I'll be all alone again!
I don't think I can bear it. Just when I thought
things couldn't get any worse."
He turned away,
as big, fat tears
rolled down his
broad face.

"Oh dear, please don't cry, Roojoo," Knitbone woofed quietly, his tail between his legs. He knew exactly how Roojoo felt; hopeless and worn out with trying. The idea of having to carry on without any friends as well was really, truly terrible. "Don't worry, we'll think of something, won't we, everybody?" He looked round at the gathered group and then back to Roojoo. But the sad tiger had already slunk back into the shadows.

Chapter 16

GHOSTLY GUARDS

Together, the Beloveds and Winnie heaved the book back to the house, ignoring the queue of visitors trickling into the grounds, and the official-looking van parked in the driveway. Everybody was in a bit of a grump because, despite their best efforts, they'd managed to make Roojoo even more miserable.

There was a lot of man-guffawing and "ho-ho-ho-ing" coming from the hallway, where Lord Pepper was deep in conversation with a small man. The visitor had twinkly dark eyes and looked very smart in an expensive suit and tie. Lord Pepper, on the other hand, was again dressed as a wizard, complete with wand, stick-on beard and pointy hat.

"Ah, Winnie! You look like you could do with some cheering up! Come and meet the delightful Mr Chattergee of the National Hat Museum of India."

The man held out his hand and Winnie shook it distractedly. Ah yes, the priceless hat jewel. "Hello, Mr Chattergee."

Lord Pepper, enthusiastic as ever, continued, "This charming gentleman has brought with him the legendary Eye of Mumbai, ready to add to our glorious collection of titfers."

"What are these 'titfers' of which you speak?" asked Mr Chattergee, clearly confused.

"You know, old chap, Cockney rhyming slang – 'tit for tat', it rhymes with hat!"

"Oh, Lord Pepper, you are so knowledgeable."
Mr Chattergee patted Lord P on the arm. "This is
why I knew that Starcross Hall would be perfect.
And not only this, you have such a sense of
humour."

Winnie raised a curious eyebrow, hoping Mr
Chattergee wasn't referring to her father's outfit.

Mr Chattergee continued, "For example,
when I asked you about your security
arrangements, you said that you 'didn't have any'!
Oh, I cannot tell you how we laughed back at the
museum. 'That man is SO cheeky,' we said.
We certainly wouldn't offer anyone the Eye
of Mumbai unless they had a state-of-the-art
security system. Of course, you must have tip-top
security – *you are an English lord*! Oh, you really
are so very, very funny!"

The little man laughed and laughed until
tears rolled down his cheeks. "You Peppers *laugh*
in the face of criminals! Back at the museum I

cannot tell you how much we worry and fret that Magpie McCracken, the notorious jewel thief, will steal the Eye from right under our noses. Your positive hattitude is an inspiration. Oh look – you see? Now *I* have made a little joke! Haha!"

Lord Pepper laughed too, only rather more nervously, his eyes darting about the hallway.

146

Mr Chattergee finally managed to stop laughing, just in time for a pair of security guards to arrive from their van outside. They were dressed in black and were wearing helmets. They didn't really look like the sort who liked to joke. The two guards carefully set down a glass box. In it, on a cushion, sat a brilliant yellow silk turban. Pinned in the centre was a dazzling brooch: the majestic, glaring, glittering Eye of Mumbai. Orlando scampered up and pressed his little monkey face to the glass. He let out a big, blissful sigh, "Eez a royal-ruby sparkler! Shiny-*shiny*-shiny."

"So, Lord Pepper," declared Mr Chattergee, wiping the last few tears of laughter from his eyes with a perfectly white, crisp handkerchief. "It is time to take us to your high-security room. I cannot wait to see it."

There was a long, difficult silence whilst Lord Pepper tried desperately to think of something.

"Well, *this* is awkward," whispered Gabriel behind his wing.

Winnie sighed. First Roojoo, and now this. Today was going from bad to worse. *Somebody* was going to have to do *something* and, as usual, it was going to have to be her. She stepped forward. "Please follow me, Mr Chattergee."

"What's she up to?" asked Valentine, but the others just shrugged.

"What do you think you are doing, Winnie?" hissed Lord Pepper, scampering after her. "We don't HAVE a high-security room! Even the toilet door doesn't lock – it's wedged shut with a shoe!"

Winnie led the way down the corridor to the room called "Hats with the WOW Factor".

Mr Chattergee and the security guards followed her in and looked around. It was a bit empty. In the corner there was a Norwegian wooden headdress in the shape of a whale, a gladiator's helmet, a Native American war bonnet and an umbrella hat from the pound shop. The guards placed the glass box warily on a table and stood either side, scanning the room.

Winnie cleared her throat. "Ahem. Here at Starcross Hall, despite our collection of fascinating and priceless hats, we do not have a normal security system. We do not have tripwires or lasers or alarms. In fact, to the untrained eye, it may appear that we have no security system at all."

Lord Pepper picked the 99p sticker off his wand, looking shifty.

"Instead, we favour a more traditional approach, using methods employed by ancient civilizations."

The Beloveds were intrigued. What was Winnie playing at?

Mr Chattergee scanned the floor and the ceiling but could only see a few cobwebs, a discarded dribbling juice carton and an empty ginger biscuit packet. He frowned. "No alarms? No lasers? May I ask, Miss Winnie Pepper, what *exactly* the traditional approach you are referring to is?"

Winnie took a deep breath and gave a very deliberate wink. "Ghosts, Mr Chattergee." She cleared her throat and continued. "Guard dogs are quite normal, aren't they? Well, what about a *ghost* guard dog?" she winked again heavily. "Wouldn't that be even better? What about a ghost guard GOOSE?" Finally, Knitbone understood what was going on and wagged his tail.

"Winnie," hissed Lord Pepper, flushing beetroot red. "Now's not really the time for your imaginary friends."

Mr Chattergee turned to Lord Pepper. He wasn't smiling any more. "I can see that I am wasting my time here. Perhaps you do not understand. We are talking about *Magpie McCracken* – a professional criminal who is wanted in thirty-two countries across the globe. Nobody even knows what Magpie McCracken looks like – he could be anyone! We are dealing with a supremely clever master criminal who has been responsible for some of the most valuable objects in the world vanishing into thin air, leaving nothing behind but his trademark signature on a business card."

Mr Chattergee looked very serious and wagged his finger crossly at Lord Pepper. "The Eye of Mumbai – this priceless jewel – is now his number one target. A treasure of this quality is MUCH too valuable to be left in any old..." He broke off, noticing a small puddle appearing on the floor.

Winnie gasped. "Naughty dog! Goodness, Mr Chattergee, I do apologize. Accidents happen!" Knitbone winked at Winnie from behind the door and hid the leaking lemon squash carton in the bin. The rest of the ghosts caught on and suddenly the air was filled with rushes of air, as Gabriel flapped his great white wings.

The security guards began thrashing about, swiping at nothing, the whites of their terrified eyes visible through their visors. Orlando and Martin pinched their bottoms, steamed up their visors and tied their shoelaces together, resulting in a panicky pile-up.

For big strong security guards, they made a lot
of squealy noises.

Valentine picked up the umbrella
hat and flung it across the room
like a frisbee.

Knitbone licked Mr Chattergee's ear and
then breathed biscuit breath all over him for
good measure.

Thankfully, Lord Pepper had no idea what
was going on. In fact, he had withdrawn to his
"happy place" in his head, humming a song
about kippers, his eyes tightly shut – waiting for
the whole sorry affair to be over.

Mr Chattergee, however, was wide-eyed with excitement. "Inspiring! Incredible! I have never seen anything like it. You are doing remarkable, groundbreaking work here, Lord Pepper! We MUST have a system like this installed in our museum in India. What a wonder this is, harnessing the spirits. Please forgive me for my ignorance – the Eye of Mumbai is in safe hands here!"

After signing some official-looking papers, the Peppers waved goodbye to Mr Chattergee, who sat in the front seat of the van next to one of the security guards carefully cradling the Bristol Bobble Hat.

As they drove away in a cloud of dust, Lord Pepper patted Winnie on the back. "Phew! That was close, eh? Don't know what you said to the chap, but he seems happy as a lamb. Well done, Winnie!" He frowned. "I do hope they take good care of the bobble hat. It IS rather special."

Then he lifted his nose and sniffed. "And now, if I'm not very much mistaken, that smells like your mother's Limpet Pie. Yummy. I'm starving after all that hoo-ha."

"Well done, everyone," said Winnie, watching her father disappear back into Starcross in the direction of the kitchen. "Quick thinking."

Knitbone growled. "Magpie McCracken sounds pretty clever, though."

"We don't really have to watch the Eye all the time, do we?" whined Martin.

"No, I shouldn't think so," smiled Winnie. "Just the occasional check will be fine. It's not as if a famous jewel thief is likely to turn up in Bartonshire. It's not exactly New York!"

Knitbone sighed. "If only it was that easy to sort out Roojoo."

Chapter 17

BAD EGGS AND SPINDLY LEGS

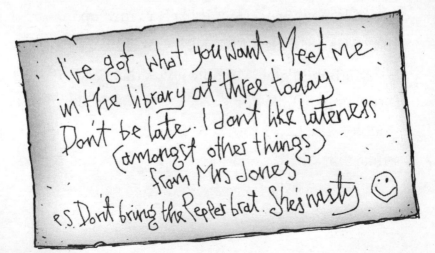

The Beloveds trudged up to the attic. As they opened the door, Knitbone spotted a note stuck to the boiler in the corner of the room.

I've got what you want. Meet me in the library at three today. Don't be late. I don't like lateness (amongst other things)
from Mrs Jones
P.S. Don't bring the Pepper brat. She's nasty ☺

Knitbone growled. "*Mrs Jones, the spider?* As in Mrs Jones, the traitor who lives in the Chinese vase? A smiley face? What a nerve!" Mrs Jones had not been very nice to the Spirits of Starcross. Knitbone's tail stood straight up in the air and he barked crossly. "How *dare* she be so rude about Winnie. Has she forgotten that she ratted on us to that horrible ghost-hunter Krispin and nearly made us homeless all for the sake of a few pink wafer biscuits? Dogs do NOT approve of disloyalty." Knitbone was working himself into something of a state. He turned his back on the note in protest.

"What exactly IS Mrs Jones anyway? Is she a Beloved?" asked Winnie, a bit confused.

"No," muttered Valentine, "she's a different sort of ghost. A 'Bad Egg'. They're nothing but trouble." The hare's brow darkened and he stroked his ears thoughtfully.

"What does she mean 'I've got what you

want'?" asked Martin, inspecting the note. "And why do you think she wants to meet us?" He gave a little shudder. "It's just that I'm not very good with creepy-crawlies."

They passed the time getting stuck into a fierce game of Snakes and Ladders and trying not to think about the task that lay ahead. All too soon, Orlando pointed at the clock. It said five to three. "Look! Eez meanie spider o'clock time! No time for chit-chat. Heave ho, m'hearties. Yo-ho-ho and a bucket of custard!" The monkey opened the attic door and dived down the stairs.

Knitbone looked up at Winnie, his eyes full of concern. She patted him on the head. "Don't worry about me, Knitbone – just find out what Mrs Jones wants. It might be important. I think I'll go and have a chat with Bertie, maybe get a bit of background on Roojoo. Anything that might help."

The library was very quiet. Visitors only came
in by accident, occasionally getting lost on the
way to the toilet. It was one of the rooms that
hadn't been done up for *Hats Off to Starcross*
and was in its original "Pepper" state, with a
threadbare carpet and moth-eaten curtains.
It was also full of some of the most remarkable
old books in the country.

The clock on the mantelpiece chimed loudly.
The Beloveds sat on the hearth, waiting. Three
o'clock precisely.

"Mrs Jones, are you there?" growled
Knitbone.

A thin scratchy voice came from behind the
clock. It sounded rather like a fork being scraped
across a dinner plate. "About time too."

A spindly grey spider crept out and perched
on the top of the clock. She peered at the group
and pointed at them with one long, hairy leg.
"Nice to see you've not brought that nasty human

with you. Stinks of
rainbows and
sunbeams *she* does."
Knitbone forced
himself to
stay calm.

"Anyway, listen up, losers. I know that you need page 84…and guess who's got it? TOO SLOW! It's me, beautiful, *special* me." She did a weird little victory dance and sang a tuneless dirge.

The Beloveds gasped in horror. What a rotter!

"Tut tut tut," chided Orlando, wagging his finger. "Missis Jones, you is selfish, nasty, stinky egg."

"Boohoo," Mrs Jones pretended to sob, rubbing four of her eight eyes. "Whatever. You might have noticed that I'm not the caring and sharing sort, which is why I pinched it in the first place. It was very disappointing when Knickerface Pickle and Whiney Winnie stumbled on how to get back together by accident because all that misery was very entertaining."

"But I *knew* that page 84 would be worth something one day. I've been watching you with that big crybaby cat. You need me, you do. I've got the answer and now I want to swap it for something else because..." she took a deep breath and closed her eyes, "*that* is what friends *do*."

"Friends?" asked Knitbone, his jaw hanging open. "I beg your pardon?"

"Yes, *friends*. That is what we are going to be,

because *now* I want to play Beloveds, just like you, on account of how brilliant I am. I'm fed up with being on my own in that vase with nothing to do but knit cobwebs. Why should you have all the fun? You bunch of no-hopers with your silly games and special gang. I demand my *own* human and then I will be just like you. Only much better obviously, because I'm *me*."

It was one of those rare moments when the friends were lost for words. Gabriel gave a squawk of outrage, folded his wings and turned his back.

"Fine. Be like that!" shouted Mrs Jones, waving her legs in anger. "Maybe I WON'T let you have page 84 after all. Actually, on second thoughts, I think I might set fire to it after tea anyway. It gets chilly in the vase."

With this she blew a raspberry and began to crawl back behind the clock.

Knitbone had a brainwave. "No, Mrs Jones, wait!" he barked, surprising everybody. "I'm sure we can sort something out. Perhaps something… better."

Mrs Jones stopped and swivelled around with a scowl. "Like what?" she spat, in a vinegary tone.

"Biscuits!" blurted Knitbone. "And not just any old biscuits – *exotic* biscuits! How would you like to own –" he leaped over to one of the bookshelves and whipped out a round tartan tin from behind a set of encyclopaedias – "*a big tin of Edinburgh shortbread?*"

Martin let out a horrified shriek. How did Knitbone know about his secret shortbread? Valentine sat on top of him heavily to muffle his cries.

"Shortbread, you say? I've not had any of that before. Is it delicious?" Mrs Jones eyed the red tin greedily. It had a very attractive picture of a castle and a little black Scottie dog on the front. It didn't take her long to come to a decision. "Give it here." She kicked a crumpled page from behind the carriage clock and it began to drift to the floor. "There. Take your stupid scrap of paper. Now stop bothering me and get lost."

"Orlando, grab it!" Knitbone barked.

Orlando leaped up and grabbed it mid-air as everyone cheered and clapped. Knitbone took it from the monkey and smoothed it out on the floor. With a big wag of his tail, he read the words to himself. "So THAT'S the answer – and it would seem we've found it in the nick of time too."

Chapter 18

ANiMALs AND ANSWERS

Winnie sat on a bench in the circus tent. In her hand she held the Circus Tombellini postcard that had plopped onto the doormat three days before. She inspected the front of it closely. In the background of the black and white picture, she could see the audience on their feet, roaring their applause. The magnificent tiger was definitely Roojoo and, despite the passing of the years, the dark-haired young boy beside him was unmistakable too.

Bertie Tombellini was sweeping sawdust from the doorways in his smart waistcoat, his shirtsleeves rolled up. It took a couple of minutes before he noticed Winnie in the stands.

He stood up and rubbed his back. "Winnie!" he smiled, running a hand through his now snowy-white hair. "How nice to see you. I'm just sweeping up ready for tonight's performance." He noticed her putting the postcard hurriedly into her pocket. "Now, what is it you have there?"

Winnie took it out again and smiled sheepishly.

"Ah, *Signorina* Pepper, you don't give up, do you?" Bertie sighed. He wandered over to her shaking his head, and sat down on the bench. "You would like to know why we have a tiger on our postcard when we have no animals at Circus Tombellini, yes?"

Winnie nodded.

Bertie took the card and looked at it hard.

"I was just a young boy when my father brought little Roojoo to me. Our circus tent was pitched in India for the winter. A tiny tiger cub, he had been found wandering in the jungle, hungry and alone. He was so small I could fit him right inside my pocket. You would not imagine it to look at him there, would you?"

Bertie absent-mindedly stroked the picture with his thumb. "He grew enormous on love and patience and mountains of spaghetti Bolognese. Then one day my papa, he say, 'Bertie, tigers belong in the wilderness, not with humans. Roojoo must go home.' So Papa chased him back into the leafy jungle. This was the right thing to do, but I was very sad.

"But hey! Guess what? The next morning Roojoo was waiting at the doorway of the tent, calling for his spaghetti!" Bertie chuckled. "My papa, he give up trying in the end. He did not need to worry because Roojoo knew where his home was. He became a member of the Tombellini family and we made up our own act – *Boy and the Mighty Rajah!* We were circus soulmates and loved playing our games together.

"Over the years we travelled the world – Australia, America, Sweden, China, Greenland – and played to sold-out audiences. He became very famous because everybody loved the Mighty Rajah and the Mighty Rajah loved them. When I put my head in his jaws the crowd went wild!" Bertie smiled. "If only they knew I did it every night when I cleaned his teeth. He grew too big for my trailer of course, so in the end we made our home in the circus tent where he could roar without rattling the china. To the audience he was savage – *the Mighty Rajah*, but Roojoo was just pretending." He took his wallet out of his pocket and showed Winnie a photograph entitled "Happy Birthday!" In it, Roojoo's delighted face glowed in the candlelight, a tiny party hat perched on top of his huge head and his whiskers draped in streamers. "He did love a party," sighed Bertie. "He was truly as gentle as a kitten and never really grew up.

Happy Birthday!

Nothing made him happier than a bedtime story. He was my *piccolo gatto* – oh, how you say in English? Ah yes, 'My little cat.'"

There was a long silence as Bertie put his wallet back in his pocket.

"Then what happened, Bertie?" asked Winnie quietly, sensing something awful. "What happened to Roojoo?"

Bertie's eyes seemed to glaze over. "Fifty years ago, in the centre of Paris, we opened on a very stormy evening. The tent was battered by gales and lashing rain, but we circus folk always say that the show must go on. People had come from all over France to see the Mighty Rajah and we could not let them down."

"Inside the tent, our performance went ahead as usual. We jumped through hoops, throwing and catching, chasing each other around the ring. Everyone was cheering and clapping, when all the lights started to flicker and suddenly went out, plunging the tent into complete darkness. *Disastro!* The crowd began to scream, when I heard an enormous roar and felt Roojoo's huge paws on my chest, sending me flying across the arena. Then there was a thunderous crash."

"Oh no!" Winnie raised her hands to her mouth.

"When the lights came up I immediately saw two things. One was a huge, heavy stage-light that had crashed to the floor from the roof of the tent, exactly where I had been standing. The second..." Bertie stopped and dabbed at his eyes. "The second was Roojoo, lying lifeless in the sawdust." He turned to Winnie, his eyes full of tears. "He had such good night vision, he must have realized that the light was going to fall on top of me. My beloved Roojoo saved my life and I never even got to say thank you."

Bertie got up to leave. "So you see, Winnie

Pepper, we do not have any animals at Circus Tombellini. Roojoo was our first and last circus tiger. No animal will ever be more special to me than him. No living creature would ever be able to replace him. He was my dearest friend. I suppose it is silly to have him on our postcards, but that way he can live on for ever."

"Oh, Bertie, what a sad story. You must miss him awfully."

"Yes, Winnie Pepper. I do." Bertie dabbed at his eyes with a handkerchief. "Nothing is the same without him at my side." He took out the beautiful gold pocket watch from his waistcoat and flipped it open. Winnie could see that it had a painting of Roojoo as the clock face, and the hands were made to look like whiskers, ticking around.

"I had this made in Vienna, to celebrate his birthday. Whenever I look at it I think of him and the happy time we had together."

Bertie cleared his throat and blew his nose. "There is so much to sort out before tonight's performance," he said, clicking his watch shut and tucking it back into his pocket. "It doesn't do to dwell on the past. Nothing can be done about it now, and what's done is done. Goodbye, Winnie."

Bertie disappeared backstage, behind the silver-starred velvet curtains. Winnie turned her gaze to Roojoo, who had been listening throughout from beneath the benches, his head in his paws. This was too awful for words. No wonder they were both so heartbroken.

Suddenly, the rest of the Beloveds burst into the tent, full of beans, popping the unhappy atmosphere like a balloon.

"What's with all the gloomy faces?" cried Valentine, looking at Roojoo and Winnie.

"Yes," squeaked Orlando kissing Roojoo's forehead. "Cheery up! You lookin' dead miserable! Hahahahahaha!" He poked his head down Roojoo's ear and bellowed, "We is *very* clever monkeys."

Martin was still sulking about his secret shortbread. He kicked up tiny clouds of sawdust moodily. "Yes," he muttered. "Apparently something really good has happened."

"Guess what?" honked Gabriel, unable to stretch out the suspense. "WE'VE GOT PAGE 84!"

Roojoo slowly took his paws away from his face, his eyes wide in amazement. "What? Really? You have the special page? Page 84? Really-really?" He leaped up. "Oh my heavens! Golly gosh! What does it say?"

His tail wagging happily, Knitbone smoothed out the page, cleared his throat and began to read aloud:

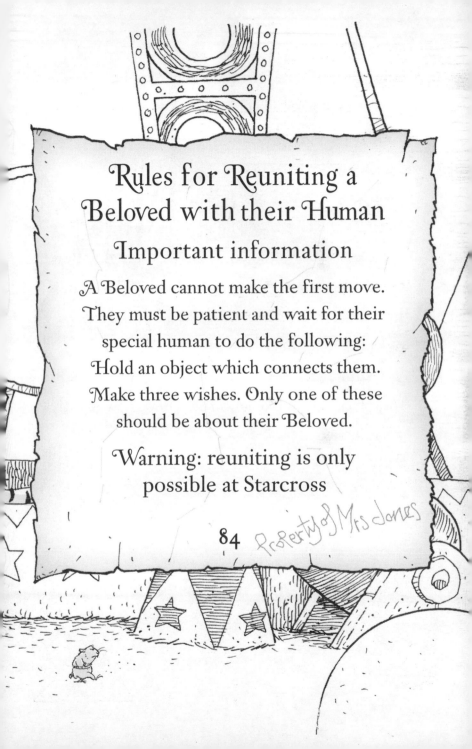

Rules for Reuniting a Beloved with their Human

Important information

A Beloved cannot make the first move. They must be patient and wait for their special human to do the following: Hold an object which connects them. Make three wishes. Only one of these should be about their Beloved.

Warning: reuniting is only possible at Starcross

84

Property of Mrs Jones

"So THAT's it!" remembered Winnie, smacking her forehead. "Of course – I had Knitbone's pumpkin collar!"

Roojoo's whiskers drooped and his jaw dropped. "Are you sure it says 'Only at Starcross'? Because the circus will be gone by morning."

"Don't worry, Roojoo, we'll do it tonight after the performance," woofed Knitbone. "First things first though. Think carefully. What is the special object that connects you to Bertie?"

Winnie and Roojoo looked at each other and their faces lit up like lanterns. They knew exactly what it was.

Chapter 19

ALL PAWS TO THE PUMP

That afternoon, Starcross was busier than ever. With the double attraction of the Eye of Mumbai and the circus happening on the same day, Winnie and the Beloveds' list of jobs seemed never-ending. As excited as they were, they barely had a moment to think about that evening's plan.

Winnie toiled away in the souvenir shop (*Titfer Tat*), filling bags with goodies and handing out badges to the visitors. They sold everything a tourist could possibly want to remind them of their special visit to Starcross. Pencils, rubbers, notebooks, wind-up chattering teeth, rulers, torches, slappy-wrist things and, of course, mood rings. There were cuddly hats, *Pantry Pirates* recipe books, postcards, keyrings and pencil sharpeners. There were spooky-looking posters of the house and T-shirts that said "Hat's the Spirit!" and "Eye ♥ Starcross Hall". The till rang all afternoon.

Meanwhile, people queued down the hallway to see the Eye of Mumbai. The ghosts haunted everyone silly, tickling babies, fiddling with hairdos, letting off stonking stinks while occasionally checking on the Eye and searching for any sign of Magpie McCracken. They were busier than bees in springtime.

Every hour, on the hour, Lady Pepper banged the gong and the queue shuffled forward into the "Hats with the WOW Factor" room, where Lord Pepper gave a talk to open-mouthed tourists.

"Welcome to *Hats Off to Starcross* – we are *beret* pleased to meet you, haha! The star of this particular room is, as you know, the Eye of Mumbai, a 56-carat ruby and a rare turban ornament. Over the years, the Eye of Mumbai has travelled all around the world and we are very proud to have it here at Starcross Hall, even though it is only for a few days."

Someone in the crowd put their hand up. "How much is it worth?"

Lord Pepper scratched his head. "Um, about £17 million, I think."

The crowd oohed and ahhed as cameras clicked and flashed.

"I've read in the papers that the famous jewel thief Magpie McCracken is after it," an old lady in the second row piped up. "How do you keep something so valuable safe?"

Lord P just tapped the side of his nose. "Our little Starcross secret," he said, wiping the nervous sweat from his brow.

When the talk was finished and the questions were over, the visitors obediently trickled into the next room ("Hats With Interesting Stains"), chattering and laughing. But one person stayed behind to have a closer look at the jewel – the elderly lady who had asked about security. She was wearing an enamelled brooch shaped like a Big Top and a copy of *Circus Fanzine* poked out of her handbag.

"It's a remarkable treasure, isn't it?" said Lord Pepper, making conversation and gesturing at the glass cabinet. Nodding, the lady unwrapped a boiled sweet and popped it in her mouth, rattling it around her false teeth.

She pushed her spectacles up her nose.
"I must say, Lord Pepper, I'm having *such* a lovely day here at Starcross. I couldn't believe my luck when I read that I would be able to visit two of my favourite things in the same place: a circus *and* the Eye of Mumbai." She took his hand in hers and gave it a pat. "My dear, it's a dream come true. You've made an old lady very happy."

Lord Pepper glowed marshmallow-pink with pleasure as she shuffled off into the next room, clutching her crocodile-skin handbag.

And if Lord Pepper hadn't been so busy grinning like a loon, he might have noticed that her bag was embossed with four gold letters: M. McC.

Chapter 20

BiG NiGHT OUT

That night, the air was charged with
expectation. *Hats Off to Starcross* was
a massive hit, it was the final night of the circus
and Roojoo and Bertie might be together again
at last. The Beloveds and Winnie declared it a
"Big Night Out" and they all decided to dress up
as it was a special occasion. As no one but
Winnie could see them, the Beloveds could wear
whatever they fancied.

The ghosts rummaged through Winnie's

dressing-up box, pulling out all manner of treasures. "What are you going to wear?" asked Winnie, choosing a cowboy costume.

"Don't look," woofed Knitbone, bounding around excitedly, "then it will be a surprise…"

Ten minutes later Winnie stood patiently waiting, hands over her eyes. "Are you ready yet?"

Martin squeaked, "Erm…yes…no…okay, you can look now. Ta-daaa!"

Winnie lowered her hands and tried very hard not to laugh.

Valentine had draped himself in a black velvet cloak and popped on a top hat over his long ears. He was wearing a joke nose-and-

glasses set. Gabriel had chosen a long white
dress, complete with veil. Together they looked
like a bride and groom.

Martin had wrapped
himself in a yellow
feather boa, and
looked just like
a fat baby bird.
Knitbone wore an
evening jacket, a pirate
hat, an eyepatch and

a tutu. He had cocked
the hat at a slight
angle, as if he
might look
more
mysterious
that way.

Winnie
stifled a giggle.

"You all look amazing. But where's Orlando?" The little monkey tottered into the attic. He was wrapped from head to tail in silver foil, with only his eyes and toes peeking out.

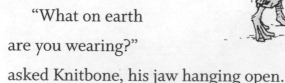

"What on earth are you wearing?" asked Knitbone, his jaw hanging open.

Orlando squeaked in outrage.

"Can't you tell?" giggled Winnie. "Orlando is a SPOON, of course!"

Orlando added, a tad sulkily, "Spoons love the circus. Everybody say so."

"Of course they do," crooned Winnie, giving Orlando a big hug. "Right, everybody, are we ready then? It's showtime!"

The crowds were making their way into the circus tent. Bunting fluttered in the evening breeze and the coloured fairy lights draped over the entrance twinkled like tiny fireflies. Jumbling and bumbling, shuffling along, the people were all keen to find their seats and enjoy Circus Tombellini's last night at Starcross Hall.

Winnie and her companions shuffled past knees and handbags, magnificent in their fabulous fancy dress. Winnie pointed to good seats on the back row and settled down.

"Isn't that Mrs Jones over there?" said Gabriel, pushing aside his veil and craning his long neck to see down to the front row. "She looks even more upset than usual."

The grey spider was clinging to the end of a bench, blubbing and wailing, sobbing her eight eyes out as if it was the end of the world. On closer inspection they could see that she was sat on a pile of shortbread crumbs.

"So shortbread makes ghosts miserable. Fancy that," tutted Knitbone. "That was a narrow escape, eh, Martin?" The hamster looked sheepish. "Let's stick to reliable biscuits in future, shall we?"

With a knowing smile at Knitbone, Winnie pulled a picnic basket out from under the bench and placed it on her lap.

"What's that?" asked Valentine.

"It's a surprise picnic," explained Knitbone. "I saw it on television – people bring snacks to the circus." He opened the hamper and Martin, thrilled, clapped his little pink hands. In the basket lay an assortment of ginger biscuits in lots of different shapes and sizes. There were little stars decorated with icing, ginger curls, not to mention de luxe ginger creams. There were even a few pink wafers in case of "emergencies". Martin clambered onto the wicker edge and balanced on his tiptoes. He stretched up to the

skies and without further ado dived headlong into the basket's gingery depths.

In the front row, Lady Pepper handed Lord Pepper her binoculars.

"Is that Winnie over there?" she asked.

Lord Pepper held them up to his eyes and squinted into the stands. There, on the other side of the arena was Winnie. She was sitting by herself on the back bench, seemingly all alone.

"Do you think she's alright?" He bounced up and down in his seat, waving his arms and calling, "Yoo-hoo! Winnie darling! We're down here." But Winnie just nodded and smiled.

Lady Pepper sighed and looked down at her boots. "She spends so much time on her own these days since…you know…since…" They still couldn't say the words, even after all this time. Knitbone had meant the world to them, but being optimistic sorts, the Peppers were all at sea when it came to dealing with sad feelings. Lady Pepper clasped Lord Pepper's hand tightly.

"Nothing lasts for ever, I suppose," said Lady Pepper. "But we must remember that tonight is a happy night. Now," she said, blowing her nose loudly and sitting up straight, "where's that Volcano Popcorn?"

Chapter 21

THE ROBBER
AND
THE RUBY

The first half of Circus Tombellini's final
night at Starcross was thrilling. The crowd
clapped and cheered as the acrobats see-sawed,
leaped and flipped. They gasped at the sword-
swallowing and were on the edges of their seats
when the juggling tightrope-walker wobbled.
Evangelina's fire-breathing was remarkable, and
when Mario the Strongman balanced her one-
legged on his outstretched hand, she seemed as
light as a feather. Finally, the clowns came on

and hurled buckets of confetti into the audience
and everyone squealed with joy.

When the lights went up for the interval,
the atmosphere was charged with excitement.
Mums and dads rummaged in their pockets for
change as children licked ice-creams and pleaded
for more popcorn.

Roojoo, who was sitting next to Winnie,
had been sneezing all the way through
the first half. "A-tishhoo! AAAAA-CHOOO!
A-tishooo!"

Knitbone, sitting on Winnie's other side, looked over at the tiger, who was blowing his nose. *Most peculiar*, he thought, nibbling a ginger curl. *I didn't know that ghosts could get a cold. "Pawly", I suppose you'd call it. I must check that in The Book.*

"Bless you!" said Martin, spraying a cloud of crumbs over Roojoo.

"Aaaa-choo! Aaa-choo!" Roojoo's eyes were streaming.

"What's up with you? Are you suddenly allergic to sawdust?" asked Valentine, grinning and pushing his joke glasses up.

Winnie looked concerned. "I hope you're not coming down with something. We need you to be on top form later."

"It's not a cold," sniffed Roojoo, wiping his nose with his giant paw. "It must be my allergy."

The Beloveds looked at him in amazement. "Allergy?" asked Knitbone. "What on earth are tigers allergic to?"

"Well, dear friends, it is the most interestingly peculiar thing. There is…*aaa-choo!*…only one thing in the world that tickles the nose of a Bengal Tiger – and that is a genuine Indian ruby."

"How odd," murmured Winnie, "because there's only one genuine Indian ruby at Starcross and that's safely tucked away in a glass cabinet

in the house…" Winnie shot up like a jack-in-the-box. "OH NO!"

In the blink of an eye, the ghosts were hitching up their hems and galloping back to the house. They scrambled through the open door, sliding across tiles and skidding around corners, until they reached the "Hats with the WOW Factor" room.

Inside the cabinet was the yellow silk turban. But where the Eye of Mumbai *should* have been, was a calling card, neatly tucked into the turban's folds.

And on the card was an elegant signature:

Magpie McCracken.

For a moment, nobody could think of anything to say. They stared at the card in the cabinet, willing it to turn back into the stolen ruby. Needless to say, it didn't work.

"IT'S GONE! This is a disaster," wailed Winnie. "Mr Chattergee's going to be furious!" Hands over her face, Winnie paced around the room, breathing slowly, trying to stay calm and figure out what to do next.

"But we didn't SEE anybody who looked like a robber," protested Martin in defence. "Robbers have stripy shirts and wear eye masks. I've seen them in comics. They carry bags marked SWAG."

"Yes," agreed Gabriel, who had just finished reading a detective novel and considered himself to be something of an expert on the subject. "We'd definitely have noticed someone dressed like that."

Meanwhile Knitbone did a sum in his head:

Starcross – The Eye of Mumbai = Big Trouble

This was both obvious and depressing, so he did another one instead.

Tiger Tent Sneezes + Ruby = ?

Something puzzled him. If the ruby had been

taken then why was Roojoo having sneezing
fits now?

"Wait a biscuit-barking minute!" woofed
Knitbone, as the truth dawned on him. "It's
alright – *the Eye of Mumbai must still be
somewhere inside the circus tent!*"

The Beloveds ditched their costumes, picked
up their paws and galloped back to the tent with
five minutes of the interval remaining.

"Where were you?" asked Roojoo, rubbing
his nose. "I was left here sneezing all on my
own."

"Never mind that," said Knitbone, "we need
to find out exactly where your sneezes are
coming from. Do you fancy a game of *Find the
Ruby Robber*?"

Martin and Gabriel scanned the audience
for stripy T-shirts and swag bags, just in case,
but there were none to be seen. They slipped
out of their seats and all followed Roojoo around

the arena, sniffing here and there, under seats and in bags, musing on what Magpie McCracken looked like.

"I bet he's got a twirly moustache," whispered Gabriel.

"Probably a beard," growled Knitbone. "I think he's very tall and covered in tattoos. He's bound to be wearing all black too – he is a master criminal after all. We're just going to have to be dead brave. Remember, everyone, *we're* supposed to be the scary ones."

They wove in and out of the stands, squeezing past people's knees, Winnie saying, "Sorry" and "Excuse me" and "Sorry" again.

By the time Roojoo reached the second-from-the-front row, his itchy nose had gone into overdrive. "Atchoo! Aaahchoo! AAA…AAAAA… TCHOOOOOOOO!" He sniffed along the row until he came to an old lady chatting away to her neighbour. "AAAAA…TISHOOOOOO!"

The ghosts stopped. "Are you sure about this, Roojoo," said Martin, pointing, "because THAT'S just a little old lady in a cardigan?" Roojoo gave a sneeze like a bazooka gun going off.

"Thinking about it," whispered Winnie, "Mr Chattergee *did* say that no one had ever actually *seen* Magpie McCracken... Maybe he's a she, and *she's* an old lady!"

Knitbone gave the old lady an investigative sniff and raised an eyebrow. "Very odd."

"What is?" hissed Winnie.

"She doesn't smell of anything." In Knitbone's experience everything smelled of something. It was very suspicious. "Old ladies always smell of lavender, talcum powder and fruitcake. This person is definitely hiding something. An animal's nose never lies, it is very reliable like that."

Winnie slipped into the empty seat beside the mysterious old lady and began to eavesdrop closely on the conversation.

"Oh yes, I have a terrible weakness for the circus," twittered the old lady to her neighbour, "have done since I was a little girl. I love it.

I collect all sorts of trinkets, the shinier the better, but my favourites are circus knick-knacks. I'm such a magpie," she chuckled, adjusting her silk scarf. "My little flat is full of china dancing poodles and juggling clowns. Have you noticed the ringmaster's exquisite pocket watch? It's charming... I *know* I should really have got straight on the bus home, but when I heard the circus would be here, well, I simply couldn't resist. I do *love* the magicians – all that sleight of hand." She held up a paper bag of boiled sweets. "Would you like one, dear?"

Knitbone growled. "The *pocket watch*? Well she's in for a surprise if she thinks she's getting her sticky mitts on that too!"

Valentine clocked the gold initials on her crocodile handbag and nudged Orlando. With a twinkle in his eye, the monkey dived inside, rifling through crosswords, tissues and reading spectacles. After a few seconds, his head poked out. "Nope. Eye of Spoon-pie eez *not* in biteyface bag."

"I bet she's got it," whispered Knitbone. "Keep looking."

"Yes, sir," squeaked Orlando. He leaped out of the handbag, scampered up on to McCracken's shoulder and dived down the back of her cardigan.

The cardigan wriggled and Magpie McCracken shifted in her seat, vaguely aware of a rummaging sensation in her middle area, which she put down to indigestion.

"Any luck?" honked Gabriel, marvelling at the monkey's devotion to duty.

The seconds ticked by. Martin wrung his hands anxiously. "Orlando, are you alright down there? Give us a sign." A muffled squeak came out of the old lady's petticoat.

"What did he say?" whispered Winnie.

Orlando, looking very ruffled, dropped out of her skirt and crouched beneath the wooden benches. In his hands he held the glittering ruby aloft like a trophy and crowed, "Sparkle knickers ahoy!"

The ghosts shuffled to the end of the row and huddled together whispering a plan. They were back in control of the ruby, but Magpie McCracken still had her beady eye on Bertie's pocket watch. It was time to teach this jewel thief a lesson she wasn't likely to forget in a hurry.

The Beloveds stood in a circle and, looking rather like a magical animal carousel, they high-fived other with a single *CLAP!* The bell rang for the end of the interval and the lights went down. The moment had come for the Spirits of Starcross to swing into action.

"SHOWTIME!" roared Roojoo.

Chapter 22

THE GREATEST SHOW ON EARTH

Bertie stepped into the middle of the arena, standing in the bright pool cast by the spotlight. One of the acrobats started playing a flute and another, a cello. Their music was somehow secretive and beautiful, rising and falling in magical waves. "Ladies and gentlemen, children and friends, welcome to the second half of the show. It is my privilege to introduce to you a man of mystery and wonderment. What you see here tonight will amaze and astound you."

Magpie McCracken sat up straight, grinning like a monkey stuck in a bucket of bananas. The ruby was safely tucked in a special secret pocket in the back of her undergarments. Nobody ever suspected an old lady of hiding stolen goods and *definitely* not in her knickers. She could concentrate on enjoying the show, perhaps even picking up that gorgeous pocket watch as a souvenir afterwards.

"Without further ado, I give you the one, the only, the astonishing, the incredible… THE AMAZING UMBONZO!"

The arena was filled with applause.

Magpie McCracken clapped hard. The Amazing Umbonzo wore a long purple cloak lined with gold. A candelabra glowing with the light of ten candles stood to one side of him, sending mysterious shadows dancing across the tent. The audience, bewitched and breathless, waited to see what would happen next.

Bertie strode into the audience. "The Amazing Umbonzo needs a volunteer! Who will it be?" Hundreds of hands flew up, fluttering in the air like eager birds. Bertie pointed at a man wearing glasses. "What about this gentleman, Umbonzo? No?" Bertie pointed to an excited boy at the back, desperately waving his hand. "Well, how about this young man?"

Winnie stood up and pointed at the old lady along from her. "What about her?" she shouted and the spotlight swung onto the second row. For Magpie McCracken, this was the cherry

on the cake. The crowd clapped and cheered
as Bertie led Magpie McCracken by the hand,
handbag over her other arm, into the arena.

"Step up, beautiful lady," said Umbonzo. "May
I ask – what is your favourite flower?" Umbonzo
whipped out a tulip from his sleeve and winked.
"Or perhaps I don't need to!" Magpie McCracken
blushed and the crowd applauded.

"Could you tell me the time, please, madam?"
asked Umbonzo. The old lady went to check her
watch, but her wrist was bare. She looked back
at Umbonzo to see him dangling the timepiece
between his fingers. The audience cheered again
and Magpie McCracken grinned. *What a wonderful
illusionist – such an inspiring professional*, Magpie
thought to herself as she tittered and fussed with
her hair. She hadn't noticed a thing and he had
stolen it from right under her nose. Yet another
thing she hadn't noticed was the small ghost
monkey clambering up the back of her cardigan.

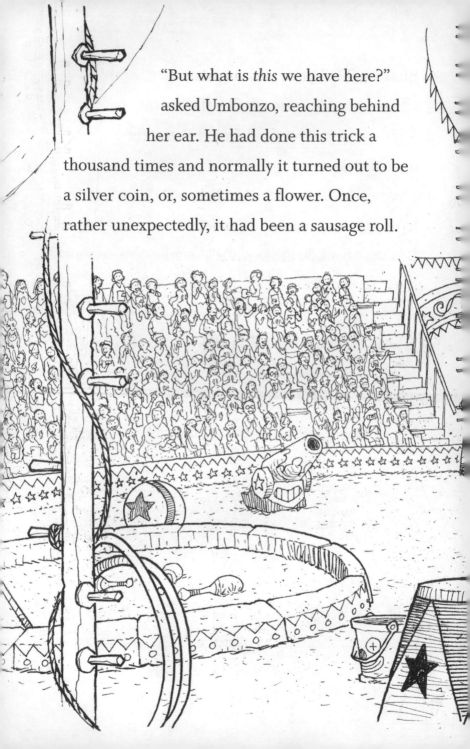

"But what is *this* we have here?" asked Umbonzo, reaching behind her ear. He had done this trick a thousand times and normally it turned out to be a silver coin, or, sometimes a flower. Once, rather unexpectedly, it had been a sausage roll.

But even Umbonzo was surprised
when a huge, glittering ruby the size of
a goose egg tumbled out from behind the
old lady's ear.

Mystified, the magician held it in his
hand and inspected it. "Oh dear. Oh my.
Um. Hang on…isn't this…?"

Lord Pepper stood up in the front row and shrieked, clutching at his hair with one hand and pointing with the other. "OH MY STARS! MY MOONS! MY DAYS! *THAT IS THE EYE OF MUMBAI! THIEF!*" Everything went very quiet except for a cello string snapping with a tuneless p-*iiing*. The crowd gasped, unsure if this was part of the show and whether they should cheer or boo.

Before they could decide, Magpie McCracken snatched the ruby out of Umbonzo's hand with the speed of a pouncing cat. *How dare he?* Her big-pants pocket was private! *It was shocking,* Magpie thought angrily, *blooming thieves were everywhere these days.* Still, she wasn't one to give up easily. Ignoring the gasps and whispers of the audience, she marched confidently out of the ring, head up, chin out, the jewel tightly in her grip.

But, striding towards the exit, with her eyes focused on the door, McCracken didn't notice Winnie's cowboy boot in the aisle, stuck out at a right angle. The old lady tripped, she flipped and the Eye slipped from her fingers flying up, up, up into the air. Instead of coming to land in the sawdust however, it stopped, suspended in mid-air, magically floating like a tiny, red planet. It almost seemed to glare down at her.

Meanwhile, Magpie McCracken lay spreadeagled in the sawdust, trying to figure out what on earth was going on.

In fact, Orlando had the ruby in both hands and was hanging upside down from a rope by his tail. For a few seconds, the jewel swung in a wide arc, side-to-side like a rosy pendulum. Then, without warning, it shot horizontally across the tent, straight into Gabriel's beak. The goose opened his wings and flew up into the roof, gliding around. The audience clapped and cheered as the jewel appeared to float in a circle.

Magpie McCracken struggled to her feet, snapped her handbag shut and hung it back over her arm with grim determination. She hadn't become an international jewel thief by giving up at the first hurdle. She didn't know what weirdness was going on here, but one thing was certain – she was going to get the Eye back.

She marched back into the arena and snatched Bertie's ringmaster whip, taking direct aim at the ruby. *CRACK!* She snapped it from the air, flicking it out of Gabriel's invisible beak with the tip of the whip. Knitbone ran into the ring and caught it in his mouth as it dropped straight down.

McCracken dived towards the jewel with
a snarl, but Knitbone had tossed it into the air
and thwacked it across the arena using his tail
like a tennis racquet and barking,
"Valentine – it's in your court!"

Valentine raced into the
shadows, leaped up and caught
it deftly between his paws. He
pirouetted gracefully and in
one fluid motion bowled it back
across the sawdust, shouting,
"Martin – to you!"

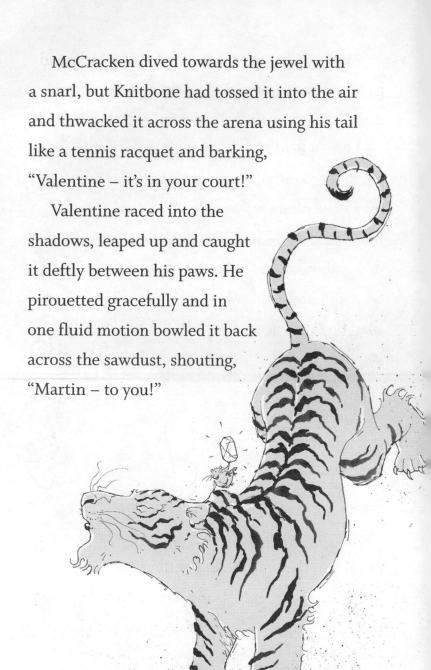

The little hamster clung to Roojoo's back and galloped past. In the nick of time, he swung down and scooped the jewel up, rodeo-style.

Martin held tightly on to the orange fur, whooping as Roojoo's sneezes transformed him into a tiger bucking bronco. "Yee-haa!" he hollered. "Hey, Knitbone! Backatcha!"

Knitbone bounded upwards, snatched the ruby in his teeth and flew through the hoops of fire, one after the other. Magpie McCracken stayed hot on his heels: seething, grabbing and ranting as they raced around the ring.

The crowd were sighing in awed joy. This was the best thing they had *ever* seen. How did

Circus Tombellini do it? They looked for hidden wires but could see nothing but thin air. The Eye of Mumbai appeared to be zinging all over the tent, levitating as if controlled by a magical unseen force. The guests didn't know how right they were.

A split second ahead of Magpie McCracken, Knitbone skidded in the sawdust and tossed the ruby back to Roojoo. With a flick of his stripy tail, the tiger sent the jewel rocketing higher and higher. The audience watched it fly like a shooting star across the dark night sky of the circus tent ceiling, before it plummeted down – *plop* – into the Amazing Umbonzo's cloak pocket.

With surprising levels of stamina for a pensioner, Magpie McCracken launched herself across the ring at the magician. "That's *mine*, you thief!" she raged, making a furious grab for the treasure.

Panicked, Umbonzo noticed baby Aldo's pram parked in the audience. He plucked the ruby from

his pocket and pitched it
straight into the soft
woollen baby blankets.
Aldo blinked his big
baby-blue eyes in
surprise. He picked it up
in his sticky fists, gave it a

happy suck, and dropped it in his lap.

Lord and Lady Pepper were on the edge of their
seats. What WAS going on? Where was Winnie?

Magpie McCracken scrambled over the front
two rows in a most undignified fashion. At last –
candy from a baby! But she had reckoned without
Aldo's mother, who was not impressed. Evangelina
blew out a torrent of fire, stopping the old woman
in her tracks.

Right on cue, the rest of Circus Tombellini,
now believing this to be an unexpected change
in the act, sprang into action. A trapeze artist
whooshed by like an eagle, swooping over baby

Aldo and snatching the Eye from the pram.

The grinning trapezist then swung up high into the roof and threw the jewel back down to one of the jugglers, who juggled it round and round. Magpie McCracken started bashing the poor juggler around the head with her handbag.

With a cry of "SNUGGLERS AHOY!" Orlando soared to the rescue of his juggling hero. He grabbed the ruby and pounced down the back of Magpie McCracken's cardigan, causing her to squawk like a startled parrot. To the audience's glee, the old lady started doing a funny, wriggly dance – this time she knew it wasn't indigestion but something a lot weirder. After a hilarious few seconds, Orlando suddenly shot like a rocket from the pleats of her skirt, and swung nimbly up onto the high wire, the Eye all the while coiled tightly in his tail.

By this point, Magpie McCracken was roaring with anger and blind with rage.

She clambered up the high-wire scaffolding, her tights wrinkling around her ankles and pulling her big knickers down too, all of which delighted the audience.

Perched on top of the spotlights, Orlando waited patiently for the old lady to catch up as she puffed and panted, determined to reach the very top. The Eye of Mumbai sat on the edge of the tightrope platform like a glistening red apple, ripe for the picking.

Exhausted, Magpie McCracken reached the top and, hooting weakly

in triumph, she stretched out a sweaty hand.
Her fingertips crept forwards towards the ruby's
priceless, sparkling facets... The crowd held

their
breath.
And
Orlando
booted it
straight

off the platform like a football.
The Eye plummeted down,
down, down into the arena,
landing neatly in Mario the
Strongman's enormous mitts. Not sure what to
do, he promptly threw it to Bertie like a hot coal,
who tossed it to Winnie, who catapulted it
straight into Lady Pepper's Volcano Popcorn,
who fished it out and gave it to her husband
who put it straight under his wizard hat for
safekeeping. *Phew!*

But the circus wasn't over yet. The crowd's gaze swung upwards as Magpie McCracken stood on top of the high-wire platform. Gritting her teeth, she knew her only option was escape. Gathering what remained of her dignity, she stepped onto the tightrope, using an umbrella in her handbag to balance her. She wobbled and bounced, high above the ground as she took a hesitant step forwards. The audience laughed and laughed at the funny old lady clown.

Martin liked guns, even glittery ones. He'd had his eye on the circus cannon for a while, wondering when he would get the chance to try it out. As the hamster stood watching Magpie McCracken, he thought that now seemed as good a time as any.

Before anyone could stop him, he had scampered over to the cannon and lit the fuse. "Bombs away, boys!"

It sizzled, it sparkled. Suddenly the cannon exploded with a terrific bang. A glitter bomb burst into the sky like a champion firework. This was too much for Magpie McCracken, who screeched and lost her footing on the thin tightrope. The crowd below gasped in horror as she slipped and floated down into the arena, umbrella in hand…straight into a paddling pool that the clowns had helpfully filled with ice-cold water. Glitter drifted all about, falling through the air like shiny rainbow snow.

As it fell, the glitter began to settle into a distinct shape. For a brief moment it seemed to form the shimmering outline of a magnificent tiger, standing on its hind legs and roaring, swiping its enormous paws majestically through the air.

Magpie McCracken sat in the paddling pool, soaked and petrified. "Did you see that?" she gibbered to the clowns as they picked her up by her arms and legs. "Did you see that…that *beast*?"

But Bish, Bash and Bosh weren't listening and parped her nose without mercy. They crammed the dripping wet old lady into their clown car and drove her across the arena to clown jail, ready to be picked up by the police, all the time honking and waving at the appreciative crowds.

In the centre of the tent, Roojoo gave a sparkly sneeze – "Aa-tchoo!" – and Winnie stroked his fur.

"A truly excellent performance from the Mighty Rajah," she said, smiling. "Possibly his best ever!" And the Beloveds all agreed wholeheartedly.

Meanwhile, the audience were on their feet, stamping and cheering with wild abandon.

Children and grown-ups flooded into the arena, mingling and dancing with the circus folk to the rousing strains of the finale music. The troupe bowed low again and again as long-stemmed roses flew about their ears, before finally withdrawing behind the heavy velvet curtain at the back of the tent.

"Bravo!" the crowd chanted, clapping furiously until their hands hurt. "Encore!", "WHAT a performance!" and "More!" They had never known a day out like it. Starcross Hall was undoubtedly the *best* tourist attraction in the world.

As the tired and contented circus-goers finally dispersed, full of candyfloss and happy memories, Knitbone looked around the tent. "Hang on, we're not finished yet. Where's Bertie? Has anyone seen Alberto Tombellini?"

But the Ringmaster was nowhere to be seen.

Chapter 23

CIRCUS SOULMATES

Alberto Tombellini was sitting in his trailer in shock. He couldn't make head nor tiger's tail of what he had just seen with his own eyes.

"Bertie, are you there?" Winnie pushed open the door and stepped into the trailer. She saw that the walls were covered in photographs. Every picture was of Roojoo – Roojoo performing, Roojoo eating cupcakes, Roojoo camping, Roojoo roaring, Roojoo being tickled.

They reminded Winnie of the scrapbook she'd kept of Knitbone. She understood how important those pictures were to Bertie. They were all he had left.

Bertie was staring at the photographs. "Winnie, don't laugh," he whispered, "but just now, *I think I saw him.*"

Winnie began arranging the photo frames neatly on the dresser and cleared her throat. "You know, Bertie, a while ago my dog died. His name is Knitbone Pepper, by the way. He's my best friend too."

"*Was* your best friend, don't you mean?" said Bertie kindly.

Winnie's eyes twinkled. "Bertie Tombellini, I think there is something you need to see…but first, do you have your special tiger pocket watch?"

"My watch?" Intrigued, Bertie instinctively reached for his waistcoat. "Well, yes, of course, but why?"

Winnie fixed him with a steady gaze and held out her hand. "Do you trust me?"

Bertie looked into her sparkling eyes. "I think I do, Winnie Pepper," he said, placing his pocket watch in her open palm.

Winnie held the watch tightly and pushed open the trailer door with her other hand. "Then follow me." Treading softly down the steps into the moonlight, she led the old man back to the circus tent.

The tent was very still. The crowds had gone home, the circus folk were drinking cocoa in their trailers and a seething Magpie McCracken had been carted off by the police. Ducking beneath the canvas door, Winnie guided Bertie to the centre of the seemingly empty arena and sat him on a stool in a pool of light. All of the Beloveds gathered around in silence, waiting for Winnie to speak.

"Alberto Tombellini," she said, placing the

pocket watch back in his hand, "if you had three solemn wishes, what would they be?"

He thought for a moment. "Well, firstly I would wish happiness to all at Starcross, of course. Then I would wish that one day we might meet again." He paused and closed his eyes, clasping the watch tightly in his grey-gloved hand. "But most of all I wish…I WISH that Roojoo – my beloved Roojoo – was still here."

The seconds ticked by on the pocket watch. Bertie slowly opened his eyes. He looked around the tent but there was nothing to see but a young girl and the silver spangles of dust drifting in the cool night air. He shook his head and smiled ruefully, his eyes bright with tears. "Oh dear, Miss Winnie Pepper. Thank you for trying but I really am a silly old fool. I don't know what I was thinking. It must have been my old eyes playing tricks on me. I have embarrassed myself. Please forgive me." He stood to leave and wiped the corner of his eye. "Now I really must go and begin to pack up. It's time for the circus to move on…"

The sound began as a tiny bubble of noise. It grew and grew and grew until a deep rolling thunder-rumble tore through the silence like a bulldozer. The roar shook the tent from its pegs to its peak. Bertie's heart stopped stock-still in wonder, his eyes as round as coins, because he knew that special sound: a wonderful song engraved on the door of his heart. With his mouth wide open he cried, "NO! It cannot be! Winnie Pepper, what is this magic?"

Winnie, ringmistress of her own ghostly circus, stepped forward and gave a low sweeping bow. "Alberto Tombellini, I give you the one, the only – THE MIGHTY RAJAH!"

Roojoo flew out of the shadows, like a fireball comet hurtling across the night sky. An explosion of orange fur, he bounded across the arena in two giant leaps and skidded to a sudden halt, his nose just centimetres from Bertie's.

"My beloved little cat!" gasped Bertie, his eyes shining, his arms held wide.

Roojoo had waited so long to hear these words. He gave an enormous roar of joy and wrapped Bertie up in a blissful cloud of tiger-hug. Then he rolled straight over onto his back so

that Bertie could give his tummy a tickle. The old friends felt like they were in Heaven at last.

Invisible to Bertie, Orlando and Martin did a little "woop-woop" victory dance, and Gabriel and Valentine hugged each other in delight. Winnie scratched Knitbone's head. "Good boy," she said and Knitbone's tail waved like a flag in a high wind. He loved it when a plan came together.

Chapter 24

HOME, BOY

Later that evening, the Beloveds stood on the dewy grass, gazing up at the twinkling night sky. They knew that the time had finally come to say goodbye to their new friends. Starcross would be quiet without a tiger to play with.

Knitbone gave a sad sigh. "Dogs don't like goodbyes," he whimpered, his tail drooping.

Roojoo smiled. "I will miss you all very, very much. I will always remember how kind you have been. You have made my greatest wish come true."

"We'll miss you too," said Winnie. "Everyone should have a circus in the garden."

Gabriel and Valentine wiped away tears.

Martin and Orlando hugged Roojoo's legs and wailed hysterically.

Bertie shook everyone firmly by the hand. "Goodbye, Lord and Lady Pepper, it has been the most extraordinary pleasure, I shall never forget

my time in such a remarkable place. It has
meant more to me than you will ever know."
He nodded at Winnie. "You were right about
your daughter, she is indeed 'simply splendid'.
Good luck with your Starcross dreams, it is
a very magical place."

He turned to Winnie and held out a grey-
gloved hand. "For you and your special friend,"
he whispered. "A small memento of our time
together." Then Bertie gave a twinkly wink,
bowed and disappeared into the tent. At his heel
was Roojoo, who turned and waved one last
time. "Thank you for everything, my dear
Beloved friends. Until we meet again,
goodbye! Goodbye!"

"Goodbye! Goodbye!"
Everyone waved frantically,
except for Winnie who was
looking down at her palm and
smiling, for in it lay the

pocket watch. On the back it was engraved in swirly letters: *Friendship is Timeless.*

When the Peppers got up the next morning, the circus had gone, as mysteriously as it had appeared, leaving nothing but specks of glitter and popcorn in the dewy grass. Knitbone sniffed the air and detected the clear, sharp smell of joy.

Soon everything was back to normal. Mr Chattergee collected the Eye of Mumbai and complimented Lord Pepper once again on his state-of-the-art security arrangements. The visitors kept flooding in and S.O.S. were kept very busy haunting and spooking. Sometimes it felt as if the whole thing had been a dream.

One Tuesday, when the summer holidays were over and the leaves were beginning to fall from the trees, Winnie was standing at the foot of the stairs, waiting for Knitbone to walk her to the school bus stop as usual. Suddenly, the letter box went *flap* and a postcard plopped onto the mat.

Popping a triangle of toast in her mouth, Winnie picked it up and inspected the card. It was addressed to Winnie and all of *S.O.S.* (which was unusual as they didn't get post). Winnie turned it over and looked at the picture. She had seen this photograph before.

"Wassat?" asked Knitbone, bounding into the hallway and jumping up and down. He gave the postcard a sniff. It smelled of ginger biscuits, sawdust and pure happiness. "It's from Roojoo and Bertie!"

The Beloveds piled down the stairs, tumbling over each other in excitement. "Really? What does it say?" asked Gabriel.

"Yes, Winnie Pepper, spill the peas," exclaimed Orlando.

She began:

Dear Winnie, Knitbone, Gabriel, Valentine, Orlando and Martin.
We are now in Germany. The gingerbread here is delicious and most energizing! I've been making new friends along the way. I've bumped into a few more Beloveds
As you say:
"A Beloved in need is a friend indeed!"
Word is getting about...
     Miss you,
       Love and hoops of fire
          Roojoo xxxxx

14.9.
DEUC

Winnie
Star
Bar

"Word is getting about?" asked Knitbone, cocking his head to one side. "What does he mean?"

"Oh, Knitbone Pepper, you silly sausage." Winnie rolled her eyes and chuckled. "I wouldn't worry too much about it." She tickled behind his ears. "I mean, *really*, even in the whole world, how many Beloveds can there be…?"

Everyone's barking mad for Knitbone Pepper, Ghost Dog

"Full of hilarity, warmth and undefeated love...
a singularly beautiful book!"
Middle Grade Strikes Back

"My time at Starcross has been
truly spectacular – in fact,
I would go so far as to say
it was MAGIC!"
The Amazing Umbonzo,
Master Illusionist & Magician

"Darling Isadora, did you see on the
interweb-thing? Knitbone Pepper,
Ghost Dog was selected by
Mumsnet as one of their
best books!"
Lord Pepper

"Winnie Pepper is a real bobby dazzler! What a star!"
Penny Farthing, top presenter of Junk Palace

"With its sweet ghost animals and ginger-nut-fuelled adventure, this charming story ticks all the right boxes."
Love Reading4Kids

"Someone needs to stop feeding those ghosts pink wafers. Pesky troublemakers!"
Krispin O'Mystery,
Ghost Hunter Extraordinaire

"I would highly recommend that you invite the Pepper family into your life and enjoy the rollercoaster of the ride that this adventure provides."
Book Lover Jo

MEET THE AUTHOR

Claire Barker is an author, even though she has terrible handwriting. When she's not busy doing this, she spends her days wrestling sheep, battling through nettle patches and catching rogue chickens. She used to live on narrowboats but now lives with her delightful family and an assortment of animals on a small, unruly farm in deepest, darkest Devon.

MEET THE ILLUSTRATOR

Ross Collins is the illustrator of over a hundred books, and the author of a dozen more. Some of his books have won shiny prizes which he keeps in a box in Swaziland. The National Theatre's adaptation of his book "The Elephantom" was rather good, with puppets and music and stuff. Ross lives in Glasgow with a strange woman, a hairy child and a stupid dog.

Collect ALL the adventures of

KNITBONE PEPPER

GHOST DOG

Meet **Knitbone Pepper,** the lovable ghost dog!

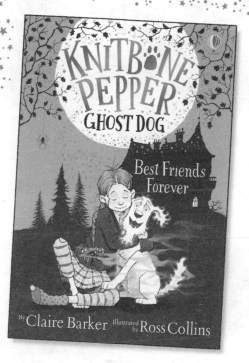

In his first adventure Knitbone makes
lots of new friends as a ghost dog.
But his owner Winnie is missing him.

Can the ghostly gang come up with a plan
in time to help Winnie see Knitbone again?

Meet Moon,
Knitbone's new friend!

One starry night, Winnie and Knitbone Pepper find a ghost horse hiding in the garden. Her name is Moon, and she is searching for her long-lost owner.

But Moon has a spooky secret in this third adventure, which is sure to spell trouble.

Look who's landed,
a human ghost!

Winnie and Knitbone Pepper are thrilled when a vintage plane lands at Starcross Hall, bringing with it Martin the hamster's beloved ghostly owner.

In this fourth adventure the visitor is a human ghost – and that means mischief!

Alakazam!
Where wishes come true...

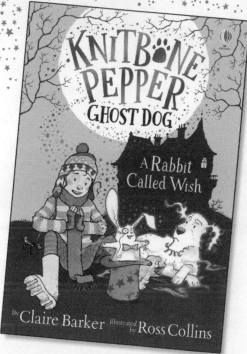

When a ghost rabbit turns up at Starcross,
Winnie and Knitbone try to help him find his
long-lost owner – a young magician called Ernest.

Can the ghostly gang put on a tip-top talent show
to entice Ernest to Starcross in this fifth adventure?